# Bloody Soaps

Novels by
**JACQUELINE BABBIN**
published by IPL Library of Crime Classics®

BLOODY SOAPS
BLOODY SPECIAL

# JACQUELINE BABBIN

# Bloody Soaps

**A TALE OF LOVE AND DEATH IN THE AFTERNOON**

## iPL

**INTERNATIONAL POLYGONICS, LTD.**
**NEW YORK CITY**

**BLOODY SOAPS**

Library of Congress Card Catalog No. 90-80760
ISBN 1-55882-064-7

Printed and manufactured in the United States of America.
First IPL edition published July 1989.
First paperback edition published June 1990.
10 9 8 7 6 5 4 3 2 1

For George Baxt, who
made this possible.
And for the A's and
B's who almost made
it impossible.

# *Foreword*

FACT:    Daytime Soap Opera is the most maligned and misunderstood of all art forms—especially by those who have never watched it. It is a complicated and rich art form, as I learned when I produced ALL MY CHILDREN for four and a half years. Though it was "the best of times," unfortunately it was *all* the times, and I wished to move on to other forms such as:

FICTION:    That is what this book is from beginning to end. *I* am not in this book nor are any of the characters or people who were involved with AMC. THE KEY TO LIFE and everyone in it has no relationship to anyone living—or dead.

# THE KEY TO LIFE

| | |
|---|---|
| Created by | Matilda Listman Ryan |
| Head Writer | Dewey Dakin |
| Producer | Waldemar Krog |
| Associate Producer | Nora Easton |
| Coordinating Producer | Gina Serpente |
| Director | Chuck Rosen |

CAST:     (in alphabetical order)

| | | |
|---|---|---|
| Dwight Edgerton | played by | Maxwell Arden |
| Bart Lansing | | Antonio Brunetti |
| Samantha Dowling | | Tracy George |
| Sally Deering Brown Cartwright | | Yancey Howland |
| Gray Lansing | | Jeff R. Landon |
| Jingo York | | Heather Leigh |
| Lily Edgerton | | Margaret List |
| Milo Sheraton | | Milo Muirfield |
| Lydia Sheraton | | Maud Sterling |
| Paulina Prater | | Zoe Zangwill (The "STAR") |

| | |
|---|---|
| Technical Director | Arnie Steloff |
| Associate Director | Gertrude von Richter |
| Production Assistant | Nicole Pastori |
| Stage Manager | Joseph Savage |
| Casting Director | Wanda Lou Bergstrom |
| Production Staff | Barbie Dixon |
| | John Krog |

| Hair Stylists | Jolie Dornya |
| | Mark Golden |
| Camera #1 | Roseann de Napoli |
| Camera #2 | Francis (Frank) Quinn |
| Camera #3 | Lester Williams |
| Stage Hand | Moe Chernin |

A United Broadcasting System Production

© 1988

and also involved:

| Clovis Kelley | Former 1st Grade Detective Homicide, NYPD |
| Alice Jones | Vice President of Daytime for UBS |
| Marti Livorski | Assistant to the Vice President |
| Patrick X. Patrick | President, United Broadcasting System |
| Victoria (Vickie) Jessup | Former Producer, THE KEY TO LIFE |
| Michael Ryan | Night Manager, Studio Three |
| Herbert Kaufman | Detective NYPD |
| Rebecca Riley | Policewoman NYPD |
| Dorothy (DeeDee) Dakin | Wife of Dewey Dakin |
| Elizabeth (Betsy) Simpson Krog | Wife of Waldemar Krog |
| Christian Krog | Oldest son of Waldemar Krog |
| Frederick Krog | Middle son of Waldemar Krog |
| David Bigelow | Head writer, THE HOUSE OF HANLEY |

# Chapter 1

When Wally Krog was murdered, there were so many suspects that the Police Department, at the suggestion of the Network, reinstated Clovis Kelley.

"Showtime!" Clovis said to his bathroom mirror, splaying his hands ala Roy Scheider. ALL THAT JAZZ. All this jazz. So they were going to use him as something more than a Public Relations recruiting poster, which was why he had quit the Department years back when he was a First Grade Detective in Homicide. He had finished writing his *History of Crime* and then used his PR contacts to turn the book into a best seller. He was on television so much that he almost became a Talk Show Host. His fifteen minutes of celebrity had made him a requirement for every television show as an advisor or consultant. It became a fun challenge to help create both crook and cop. The bodies and blood were fake but the money was not. And nobody got hurt. Maybe the viewers.

After six years in Lala Land, minus one month and one day— yes, he'd been counting—he returned to New York to write the definitive *History of Crime on Film.* As an added incentive (as if he'd needed one to leave the Land of the Fruits and the Nuts), Yancey was in New York tied into a soap opera contract. Bi-Coastal sex was for exhausted relationships. Hell, theirs was so new it didn't even have a category.

We interrupt this book, thought Clovis, to go and play real life detective again. He had to agree he was an ideal choice since he knew many of the people involved with the production of THE KEY TO LIFE and, as the releases said, he was "equally at home with police procedure and behind the scenes." Maybe a computer would be more reliable. Clovis was not sorry Wally Krog was dead. He looked forward to finding the murderer so he could congratulate him—or her.

Clovis had met Waldemar Krog, Producer, the first day he visited the set of THE KEY TO LIFE. In its fifteenth year on the air, he had never heard of the show, much less watched it until he had met Yancey Howland. He was looking forward to meeting the assorted zoo that Yancey had described to him. From long experience, he knew there were no similarities on shows. Each had a different pattern, each domain was unique. And this would be his first experience with an hour-long dramatic serial that aired five days a week, fifty-two weeks a year.

Yet, he was also aware that though the ground rules differed, there were certain givens on any *taped* multi-camera show, be it Day Time or Prime Time. The Producer, unlike in film or theater, is not a money raiser but a hired gun. The responsibilities are enormous since s/he alone is on target for holding to a stringent budget while delivering a high-rated show against all odds. Odds being an interfering Network and inexperienced or intractable creators. In charge of the "above-the-line" aspects of the show, which includes the so-called creative elements from writing to casting to design to music, s/he also supervises the "below-the-line." This includes everything from the physical plant of the Studio itself and the scenery as well as all the necessary engineering components from cameras through editing. Of course there is the hiring and firing of various personnel, tempered by Network and union rules. The Producer must balance a high rating in the Nielsen sweepstakes while handholding the Talent with all sizes and shapes of ego. The symbolic buck stopped with the Producer. It was much like being the Headmaster of a top school or the

Captain of a battleship. Power? Yes. But too few realized it was quite fickle.

Clovis strolled slowly down Columbus Avenue. He loved its bazaar feel, the crowds, the peddlers and tacky stores tucked next to each reinvented restaurant. Clothes and Cooking and Characters. The energy of New York's changing yet constant insanity. Oxymoronic. Last year's break dancing had given way to this year's Oriental-tended metal tables covered with scarves, gloves, batteries, sunglasses, hats, toys, magazines, bibles, cassettes, jewelry. Not craft fair specialists. Just utilitarian Made-in-God-Knows-Where junk.

He glanced at himself in the shop windows. Ralph Laurened from head to sock. The boots were Tony Lama Peanut Brittle. He would do Yancey proud. Yes, maybe he did care about her more than he wanted to admit even though he could not—would not —think of them as a couple. That's a name, a title, a full commitment and he was not ready for that. No way.

Turning the corner, he saw the fans jammed against each other, plastered against the glass door of the studio trying to glimpse inside. Bees against a hive. Clustered. Droning. He had to separate them physically to get to the door. In their red raincoats, hooded parkas, torn, worn jackets, they clung to the door and to the strollers filled with sticky fingered hollow eyed-kids. Blacks, Hispanics, midwestern whites yearning to catch a glimpse of their Gods as they left or entered the fingermarked doors of Studio Three. As he pushed his way through the swarm of fans, he felt their hands touch his Harris Tweed jacket. And the voices: "Who is He? What part does he play? He was on last year. Naw. Hey, Mister, who are you? He's nobody. He ain't on the show. Nobody. Ain't nobody."

Inside the entrance of the Studio was a desk presided over by a uniformed black man with a huge grin.

"Mr. Kelley to see Yancey Howland" said Clovis, trying to straighten his jacket and pockets.

The guard picked up a microphone and crooned into it. "Yancey Howland come to the lobby. Yancey Howland come to the lobby." He indicated two large gray flannel sofas flanking an oversize television set that was blaring a commercial for Lee Press-On Nails. Clovis positioned himself under the huge block letters of the show's title on the rose-carpeted back wall and studied the wide-eyed frenzy on the faces noseflattened against the door. Another force was making them part again and a short chubby woman carrying three tote bags pushed her way into the lobby.

"Gets worse all the time," she said to no one in particular. Then she headed to the door behind the guard's desk and suddenly did an about face and rushed up to Clovis. "I'm sorry if I've kept you waiting but you weren't supposed to be here until this afternoon." She dropped two totes to the floor and dug into the third one, emerging with a worn stuffed red leather engagement book and started to riffle through it. Triumphantly, she pointed to a page which she showed Clovis. "See. You're not suppose to be here until 2:30 this afternoon. I thought that's what Tex said. Anyway, I'm very glad you're here. I'm Wanda Lou Bergstrom, the casting director. So pleased to meet you." She held out a chubby hand.

Clovis shook the proferred hand. "I'm pleased to meet you. But I don't know Tex and I'm not here to see you. Clovis Kelley."

"Whoever you're seeing they'll bring you to me anyway. I do all the casting."

"I'm not an actor," smiled Clovis and sighed. Here we go again. Six foot two. High cheekbones. Rugged. Great teeth and gray-templed full head of hair. Perfect character actor. He knew exactly what Wanda Lou was registering.

"You're not an actor! I just can't. . . ."

"Hello, darling." Yancey linked her arm through his and stood on tiptoe to brush her lips against his. "No, Wanda Lou, he is not an actor. Thank God."

"Well, he should be" said Wanda Lou with great conviction, brushed her hands against the sides of her short, curled bronze hair, picked up her totes and started to go. Wheeled around and smiling took a few mincing steps toward Clovis. "Then you're . . ."

"Yes," smiled Yancey. "He's my fella."

Nomenclature. No escaping labels. Show Biz. Clovis found himself grinning back at Wanda Lou Ditz as Yancey called her.

"I wanted him to see the asylum before this inmate goes bye-bye," Yancey whispered.

"But you *can't* go," Wanda Lou's eyes widened with terror. "I'll have no one to dish with and they won't let you out of your contract and they'll sue you and things will improve and . . ."

Yancey placed her index finger on Wanda Lou's quivering lips. "Shh. This is not the place for a discussion. Come on, handsome." She tugged Clovis over to the guard's desk where he signed his name and time of arrival on a lined roster and was handed a blue laminated tag stamped "Visitor." Yancey clipped it on his jacket lapel and led him by the hand through the double doors to the right of the guard's desk. Clovis nodded farewell to a now blubbering Wanda Lou who kept dropping and picking up the totes as if she were playing a game.

"Later," mumbled Yancey as she preceded him down the deserted blue carpeted hall. "Dressing rooms." She indicated the lacquered pink doors embedded in the pink carpeted walls. Bloody padded cell, thought Clovis. She was wearing a shortie make-up smock that stopped midthigh. He stopped to appreciate the movement of her white, white legs as she strutted on impossibly high heels. State of the art.

"Stop that," she said without turning around. Taking a key from the pocket of her UBS logoed smock, she opened the door to #10. "My little home away from home. Cozy ain't it. Monks at least had windows."

"Ah, Yancey, that's where you are," said a liquid, modulated, heavily accented voice. Clovis turned to face a large well-built white-haired man, noticing Yancey's reflexive gesture to close the front of her smock. "Clovis? Clovis Kelley! Wally Krog." As Krog shook Clovis' hand, his face creased into a deep smile and the blue eyes behind the rimless bifocals sparkled. "I did not know you had a visitor, Yancey. And, of all people, Clovis Kelley. We met at the Affiliates party last year in Los Angeles. Allie. Yes, it was Allie Jones who introduced us. That was quite a presentation. I usually do not enjoy that sort of thing but that was exceptional."

I was not at that party. I never saw this man before in my life. Who in hell is Allie Jones. Why is he doing this. And what the hell does he want, thought Clovis.

"And so we meet again, Clovis Kelley." The accent with its confused Rs and Ws finally sorted itself out to be of Scandinavian origin. "He is a very famous man. Yancey, why didn't you tell me you knew him?"

"Sorry, Wally," Yancey said sharply, "it just never occurred to me that it was important to you."

"But, of course, darling, how could you know." Was the tone a trifle mocking? Clovis watched him reach for her reluctant hand and guide it toward his lips.

"Act Six. Act Six." The stage manager's voice blared through the hall. "Sheraton Library. Lydia. Dwight. Chop Chop."

"What is important," smiled Clovis, "is to put your street clothes on so I can take you to lunch."

"That will take her at least twenty minutes," Wally shared a man-to-man look with Clovis, "though she is faster than most actresses."

Before Yancey could unclench her jaw, Clovis kissed her on the cheek.

"And while you wait, why don't I show you my domain. It is a producer's perogative to be proud of his kingdom. May I?"

"Sure. Why not?" But why?

Alice Jones occupied the large corner office on the 21st floor of the United Broadcasting System's corporate headquarters. It came with the title of Vice-President of Daytime Programming. The executive-issued oak desk was not visible under the massive confusion of papers and scripts.

With the telephone securely cradled atop her left shoulder, Allie removed a tortoise-shell hairpin from her fading brown hair, swirled it through several other strands and anchored it inches from where it had been in her bird's nest hairstyle.

"Wally, I've already told you. I spoke to the 33rd floor and the answer is no. There is no way I can justify that much money for . . ." Another hairpin swirled as she listened to him oozing sincere promises of cuts and changes that would make possible the remote he wished to shoot. She continued to stare at the four television monitors side by side in the bookcase opposite her desk. Lined up in numerical order by Channel number—2, 4, 7 and 8— they were mutely tuned to the on-air programming devoted to "love in the afternoon." Four rival soap operas. As the prologues visually sequed into each classic show signature, she glanced down at the Xeroxed chart of last week's Nielsen ratings. She was in deep trouble.

"Wally, you are aware that since you've been producing KEY, it has lost its time period? And don't give me that lead-in nonsense. COMPARISONS may be a lowly game show but it still got an 8.9 rating with a 28 share. And then KEY drops to a 6.0 rating with an 18 share? Come on! One lousy remote is not going to save the show. No, Wally, forget the remote and concentrate on improving the ratings. Goodbye, Wally." Damn. How could she have allowed herself to be talked into letting Wally Krog produce anything. Much less the cornerstone show of the whole UBS Daytime line-up. Talked into it by Wally with his hand-kissing charm and the promise of his caressing male eyes. She had no one to blame but herself. Her late husband had proven that charm and talent were not synonymous. Mid-life stupidity. Two kids to put through college and only one more year on her contract and those digit heads on the 33rd floor didn't like women anyway.

The sharp rat-a-tat-tat of Marti Livorski's heavy gold wedding ring against the office door announced the arrival of her assistant. "Did you have a chance to look at the KEY outlines?" Marti asked in her precise dentalized speech that covered the gawping New Jersey accent.

Allie started to shuffle the papers on her desk, causing many of them to fall to the floor. Marti reached under the pile and pulled out the outlines covered with Allie's bird track handwriting.

"Oh, Marti, what would I do without you."

Marti acknowledged the praise by shrugging the oversized shoulders of her white Calvin Klein jacket and tossing her head so that her perfect Lulu haircut fell nicely back into place. "The story meeting is tomorrow."

"Now you tell them that they have Lydia acting out of character. She's not a teenager. She's a mature woman who has been through four marriages and has three children, as I remember. Why in the world would she be attracted to a boy young enough to be her grandson? The viewers will be offended by it and she'll lose all credibility. I'm not against her having a romantic interest but with someone closer to her own age. Or a little younger. Maybe an old school chum of Milo's? Tell those idiot writers they also have to come up with a better story line for the kids. A tenth recycle of Romeo and Juliet just isn't good enough. Don't they have any original thoughts? I think we're going to need a focus session to get them back on the track. I'll call Patrick and get him to approve the expense."

"What about the remote? Wally really wants it."

"Wally wants, Wally wants. I've told him no ten times. If he doesn't do something about bringing that show in on budget, Wally will be wanting another job." Allie peered at Marti through her light rimmed glasses as she turned away. Marti had been very eager to bring Wally on board. Was it possible that Marti and Wally? No. Today's Marjorie Morningstars like Marti didn't go into adultery. And with a husband on Seventh Avenue to keep her in all the designer clothes to which she had become accustomed, it was not likely.

"You're the boss," Marti smiled sweetly, shook her dark head and left with the annotated outlines.

Allie pushed her glasses back over the rim of her nose. Why had Marti used that phrase? Did she know something that Allie didn't? Was she making nice with the 33rd floor? Was she snaking into her job? Never. Paranoia be still. Marti would never betray her. After all, hadn't she brought her along from a typist in the pool to her assistant. She was almost as close as her daughter. Marti with her dog-on-the-grave loyalty would do anything for her. Even help her get rid of Wally Krog.

The weekly story meeting was held in Wally Krog's sparse office at the Studio where THE KEY TO LIFE was taped. Between the hours of nine and one on Friday mornings the fates of everyone in Clearview, U.S.A. were decided.

Weekly torture session was more like it, thought Tilly Ryan. Wally would read the notes Nora Easton, the Associate Producer, had prepared for him and pretend they were his ideas. Marti would read her transcription of Allie's notes and pretend they were hers. And dear Dewey, her hand-picked Head Writer, would grow rigid and squirm because even if the notes were valid, he did not know how to fix the outlines they were discussing. But that was when she, Matilda ("Tillie") Listman Ryan, would earn her $7,500 a week consultant fee and protect her $15,000 a week royalty. She was not about to let her creation, THE KEY TO LIFE, die.

As always, Wally had to make an entrance. Apologizing for being late ("Problems with the set, problems with camera #3, problems edit machine B, etcetera . . ."), he stopped short, stared at the glowing cigarette in his right hand, gave a half smile and said, "And again I forget!" He left the office to put out the offender as the others went to the same seats they always occupied. Invisible placecards determined that Nora Easton, the high strung note-taking Associate Producer, sat at one end of the long oval table and tried to protect her notes from the inquisitive eyes of Marti Livorski who sat next to her. Beside Marti was Dewey Dakin, Head Writer, who tried to take up as little space as possible with his assorted documents, charts and calendars. And next to Dewey sat Tillie Ryan.

Wally closed the door behind him and took the long way around the table so he could bend over Tillie and kiss her pale cheek. As he did, he eyed her crossed legs and murmured in her ear that she still had the best legs in New York. Tillie giggled and Wally seated himself opposite them with his back to the window.

"So, Dewey, it is the yellow tie today. The power tie?" asked Wally in his stilted accent as Dewey's hand unconsciously went to the knot and cleared his throat. "Are you feeling powerful? And Marti, you are lucky you have such a fierce animal at your front and not your back," he said referring to the huge tiger embroidered on the front of her Krizia sweater. "Do you have his tail?" Ever the personal remark. Compliment or insult? Wally delighted in the fact that most people were not sure which applied to them.

"That's not a bad sweater you're wearing yourself," smiled Marti acknowledging his grey and blue heavy knit Scandanavian.

"Want to change?" asked Wally, standing up and starting to remove his.

Marti gave a little trill laugh. Yes, she was flirting with him, Tillie noted and caught Nora's eye.

"Before we begin on the outlines, I have a note for production," said Dewey, the echoes of a southern childhood could still be heard despite a past brush with acting. "I am compelled to reiterate that Antonio's playing of Bart gets no better. He seems to be doing a Bruce Willis imitation. Bart is a sensitive boy and Antonio seems to have been allowed to get . . ."

"Now just a moment," roared Wally. "What scenes you writers

write for the boy to play? Tricks. Gags. Not one tender moment you write and how . . ."

Nora tuned out. Here they go again. She watched Tillie's wide blue eyes play a tennis match. She watched Marti doodling vapid female faces with wild hair styles. Her stomach churned and there was a bitter salty taste in her mouth. She couldn't have another attack. She couldn't afford it. Damn all of these illiterates. If only my husband were rich and capable, I wouldn't have to be sitting here listening to those two incompetents getting their kicks out of venting spleen. Her darling Bud was more man than either of them.

"Gentlemen," said Tillie soothingly. "We have a lot of work to do."

Papers shuffled and they got down to the business of going through the week's five outlines. Here a tracking problem. There a set problem. And then a time sequence to be straightened out.

"Why do we not do 4333 next?" demanded Wally.

"They're flipped," said Nora, suppressing a smile as his accent transformed all the "threes" into "twees."

"Yancey won't be here," answered Dewey in his grade school teacher's corrective voice. "You're the one who asked me if she could have the day off to do a guest shot someplace or other."

"But you never said . . ."

"We still have a great deal to discuss," said Marti, the perfect hostess into the breach. "And we still have to talk about Lydia and Buxton."

"What about them?" Dewey accused.

"Well," whined Marti, "Maybe we should rethink his age. After all, Lydia's a mature woman who has been through four marriages. Maybe her involvement should be with someone . . ." as Marti pretended to think on her feet, "someone like an old school chum of her son, Milo."

"But we agreed to that in the long story." Dewey slammed his sharpened pencil on the top of the table. "We can't go around making changes just for the sake of making changes." He reached into the worn briefcase that was beside his chair and pulled out a document and started to flip through the pages.

"Dewey," said Tillie calmly, as she patted his clenched fist, "there is a way to fix it. A college chum of Milo's is an overdone and obvious ploy from SUMMER OF 42 to SWEET SUE. However, I think we do get more mileage if we make Lydia's new love interest Dwight's long-lost brother, which can complicate the rivalry between them."

"Brilliant, my darling, as always," Wally purred at her. Marti recorded Tillie's blush.

"Another thing," said Marti, "we're going to have a focus session. Allie got Patrick to spring for it."

"Focus session." growled Dewey. "Waste of time. A group of moronic housewives from Hicksville, New Jersey who're given carfare and free bagels to sit behind a two-way mirror and answer questions about their favorite soap. Stupid frustrated halfwits giving into their fantasies. We haven't got the time for that nonsense."

"For once, for once I agree with you." Wally stood up and glared at Marti. "But time is not the question. Fuck time! They find the money for this stupid game and they don't have the money for my remote. They give me a hard time about the ratings but they won't do a remote that would bring hundreds—the hell with it!" He slammed out.

"He's just gone for a cigarette," said Nora calmly. "I better give these changes to Gina. I assume we'll resume in ten."

"Coffee," explained Marti as she left the office to find a phone to call Allie and report.

"Focus session." said Dewey pursing his lips. "We don't need that waste of time to tell us what's wrong with this show. What's wrong with this show is that man. Tillie, unless we get rid of him, we're not going to have a show at all."

"Now it's not all Wally's fault," said Tillie gently. "The network lets him have his head. I'll speak to Patrick about it. God knows, it doesn't do any good to speak to Allie. She thinks the sun shines out of his ass." She smiled at Dewey. He did not smile back. He could only see poverty ahead.

"We cannot do another remote," said Dewey, his teeth clenched in an effort to keep his voice from escalating. "Days wasted in surveys in a million changed locations and we never get caught up. We fall behind on outlines and scripts and all our planning and scheduling goes right out the window!" He tried to gather the impressive charts strewn in front of him. "As much as I hated Vickie, I wish she was back producing. At least with Vickie you knew where you stood. And she knew that a remote never got us one rating point. Yearning. Romance. Relationships. Chases and violence is for nighttime. We're LOVE." The corners of his mouth turned down, the circles under his eyes deepened and his muddy brown eyes seemed about to tear.

"Shut up!" Tillie rose, adjusting her grey and red plaid wool dress so that not a wrinkle would detract from her elegant slimness. "This is not the appropriate time to fall apart. I promise you Holly and Beau will continue their expensive schooling and DeeDee will get yet another trip to Europe this year." Dewey watched her jaw harden. She was still smiling but, it, too, was sculpted. "Don't think for one moment I'm going to let that egomaniacal prick destroy this show. My name is on that screen, too. In first position. I know how to get him. And I will."

"Who writes this shit?" Jeff Landon demanded of everyone in the rehearsal hall. Waving his script above his head, he advanced toward the production table where the Associate Director and Production Assistant sat marking changes in scripts. As Jeff started his tirade they automatically hit their stopwatches to stop timing the scene.

Chuck Rosen, the Director, who had been adjusting the folding chairs and bridge table that represented the seating arrangement in the Sheraton Library, tried to measure the intensity of Jeff's tirade. A bad one. "You are the worst." he shouted at Jeff and walked toward him slowly.

"Listen to this." Jeff demanded, " 'the both of us know what it behooves us to do so we cannot be swinging in the wind.' It's archaic garbage and getting worse."

Chuck put his arm around Jeff. An imposing blue jeaned and jacketed white-haired man, Chuck could command attention by his size alone. "If you had done your homework and read the script before this minute, we could have fixed it. But oh no! Shakespeare here has to have a temper tantrum to prove he's an actor." He got a faint whiff of booze as Jeff pulled away from him. "Don't worry, the Big Boy will fix it," he grinned.

"He always does," Jeff said wistfully. "Lemme get a cup of coffee," and, head down, leading man Jeff R. Landon left the rehearsal hall.

Maggie List, the slight, grey haired actress with whom Jeff had been playing the scene, tugged at Chuck's elbow. She led him to the center of the room away from the perked ears at the production table. "Go easy on him, he's having a rough time," she whispered.

"Wally?" asked Chuck.

She shook her head up and down, as her long loose unruly hair tumbled across her lined face. "Believe me, Chuck, that man is a plague. It's as if he's got a special radar to find the one vulnerable spot and probe it. You know. We see how he treats you. You kid him back but nobody can tell me that you enjoy those remarks about the great Tony winning director being reduced to direct a soap. And the way he mocks your technique and . . ."

"Touché!" said Chuck trying to smile. "You lie down with dogs and you get up barking. But don't tell me that he's been giving it to our lovely and lovable Lily Edgerton?" he asked, using her character name.

She looked at the mirrored walls of the room to make sure they were isolated and lowered her voice. "My contract is up in two months. I tried to see him for a month but he was always behind locked doors. And when he finally deigned to see me, he grins and says 'It's for me to know and you to find out. In a hurry to go someplace at your age.'" Her eyes filled with tears. "So I did the unforgiveable, I went behind his back and wrote Tillie a note to ask her. She assured me I was fine. She was very sweet. But, honestly, Chuck, I don't know what to believe anymore. I've been with the show fifteen years and I have two old, infirm parents who depend on me. And Penny," she added naming her yellow Labrador to try and make it all sound less desperate.

Maggie must be at least sixty, thought Chuck. "At least they live long in your family."

"Oh you." Maggie gave Chuck a grateful hug.

"Okay, let's not wait for Jeff," Chuck commanded Trudy von Richter, the Associate Director. "Let's do the next scene. Ye Olde Blueprint Cafe. Gather the troops."

Trudy headed for the phone that was hooked into the public address system to call the actors in the scene as Chuck rearranged chairs and tables to indicate the Cafe set. Maggie headed for a sofa in the far corner of the hall where she had left her knitting—a lovely teal blue alpaca sweater-to-be for Maxwell Arden who played her husband, Dwight Edgerton.

"Let me know as soon as Jeff gets back," Chuck said to the production assistant. He hoped he was really getting coffee.

The Hub. The Rumor Factory. The Hair Room. Three tall black utilitarian barber chairs faced a brightly lit wall of mirrors. Every actor visited there at least once a day. Some to pat, comb, brush, spray, mousse or just admire themselves. Others to be washed, dyed, permed, cut, wigged or curled by the two resident social directors wearing the grey UBS logoed make-up smocks: Jolie Dornya and Mark Golden.

Tiny even on the four inch heels of her backless pumps, cigarette grooved in the corner of her pouty heavily lipsticked mouth, Jolie's accent changed with the color of her hair. Basically French, its clarity depended on her emotional state of which all who entered her aura were acutely aware. Also, of the fact that anyone who sat in her chair was extremely lucky to have her expertise because she was much too good to be working on a lousy soap.

Mark, on the other hand, was thrilled, thrilled, thrilled to be working on KEY. Actually working on actors' heads rather than those dreary housewives and tacky office girls who patronized the cheap street trade salons he apprenticed after beauty school. Dark, pudgy and nervous, Mark wore his black hair in an extreme butch cut and his moustache was the in-style fag brush. Proudly, he would point out the paper on the back wall of the room: I LOVE MY HAIRDRESSER, the phrase a repeated scripted pattern in grey on rose. A gift from Mark's lover, Arthur, an interior designer.

Tracy George (Himmelfarb) watched Jolie twisting her reddish hair into hot pink rollers. "Ouch!", she complained as Jolie stuck a pin through the roller. Squinting through the cigarette smoke, she examined her handiwork in the mirror while avoiding eye contact with Tracy.

"I don't care who knows," Tracy insisted, "If that prick ever tries to snake his gross paws down my sweater again, I'm going to rip those glasses off his head and jump on them."

"Running your lines, missy?" asked Mark.

"You know damn well I'm not. The only reason he's so all fired to do this remote that UBS is fighting him on, is because he'll get another crack at me. I really feel sorry for those kids upstairs who have to put up with his shit. I wonder if I can haul him up on charges?"

"Sexual harrassment?" asked Mark as he continued to pin curl Maud Sterling's thinning grey fuzz. "With Wally's charm, he'll convince them you were after his bod."

"Don't let him get to you," Maud Sterling's cultured voice took command. She smiled at her reflection in the mirror as Mark placed the heavy dark wig on her head. She loved the way it took at least twenty years off her life. "Tracy, I've been in this business a lot longer than you. And if it isn't Mr. Krog, it will be someone else. You are a very attractive young girl." Not as pretty as I was at her age, Maud thought. Her face is too flat and that up-turned nose really makes her look like a sweet toy monkey. But she is well endowed and it was common knowledge that Wally was a tit man.

"He likes to tease," said Jolie. "Certainly, if you say no, he will leave you alone. After all, this show is a candy store for any boy who likes candy. All kinds. All flavors."

"It's a sick game with him," said Tracy. "It's a wonder he's gotten away with it as long as he has."

"I wouldn't be that sure," Jolie whispered in Tracy's ear.

"Uh huh. Jail bait." laughed Mark as Heather Leigh paused in the door. "The new kid on the block. And a brunette."

"What are you all laughing at?" asked Heather. The tall, willowy, Juilliard graduate, was still trying to suppress her Georgia accent. "Mr.—Wally said I should ask Jolie here to give me a trim before runthrough. Is that possible?"

Tracy got out of Jolie's chair and looked from Heather to Maud. "Yes, my dear, anything is possible."

"Sit," said Jolie, throwing a plastic protection cape over the girl and fastening the velcro at the nape.

"Off to makeup," Tracy announced.

"Pretty, isn't she?" Maud whispered to Mark as they examined Heather in the mirror. "Maybe I should warn her."

"Anyone seen Wally?" Johnny Krog, one of the gofers on the production staff, asked as he walked into the dimly lit Control Room.

"Wake up and smell the coffee, son," said Arnie Steloff, the Technical Director, without turning around. "This here is the

Control Room and Mr. Krog, he don't come in here most of the time. Maybe for taping. But not for runthrough. And during blocking—never." Seated at the console, facing the bank of twenty-eight monitors in front of him, Arnie continued to follow the script that had been marked by the director. He punched the electronic board of buttons with his right hand, which would move the called-for image from any of the five cameras to the large colored "on air" monitor centered in front of him.

"I've been looking all over for him," Johnny explained apologetically. "Usually he's in his office in the morning."

"With the door closed," piped up Nickie Pastori, the Production Assistant, seated at the console three seats away from Arnie. "Did you peek inside?"

"Knock it off, Nickie. Of course I looked in his office. They're having a long story meeting. No one upstairs seems to know where he is."

"Does anyone ever know where the great man is? Or what he do?" She continued to make changes in the scripts piled in front of her.

"Are you this snotty about him with everyone or is it just my luck because he's my father?"

"Poor baby. I'm just naturally like this because I can't stand unprofessional," Nickie explained.

"You know what the word means, son?"

"Stop it, both of you." Johnny clenched and unclenched his fists. "I don't want him—"

"Then why are you giving us a hard time. We have work to do if we want to get out of here before midnight."

"Look, I checked with security," said Johnny trying to keep his voice even, "and they said they didn't see him leave the building. Allie, Allie Jones is looking for him. He's holding up the long story meeting. She wants him now."

"Whee!" chortled Nickie, "maybe she's gotten the guts to fire him. The way he talks to her is something else."

"What?" Arnie was saying through his headset to Lester Williams on Camera Three. "You're supposed to be at the Sheraton Library. Shot 82. Look at your card. Okay. Okay." He deflected the lever of the Studio address system. "Chuck. Lester says he can't make it from the Bank. You'll have to stop tape."

On the Studio floor, Chuck Rosen, the Director, stood in front of the portable console where his script rested. "Punch up Three," he asked Arnie. Three's image appeared on his console. "All right. No problem. The Big Boy will fix it." He then turned to the Stage Manager, Joe Savage, and barked, "I've been waiting here for five hours and the Library set isn't ready. How many times do I have to tell you to clear the riff-raff off the set before I arrive. You are the worst!"

Joe Savage, spring-bindered script pressed against his bulging stomach, crossed over to the sofa in the Sheraton Library to remove the offending, sleeping stage hand.

"Chuck," he rasped urgently, "come here. It isn't Moe. Take a look."

In the Control Room, Arnie sensed the tension on the Studio floor. "Frank! Camera Two on headset."

"Yes, Arnie," said Frank into his headset. "What's the problem. I'm not in the scene."

"Just go see what Joe's on fire about." Arnie watched the monitor as Frank repositioned Camera Two and panned over to Joe and Chuck in the Sheraton Library. Stretched out on the green velvet sofa face down was Wally Krog. The top of a knitting needle protruded from his neck. He was dead.

Arnie pressed the P.A. button. "Take five, everybody. Take five."

# Chapter 2

Ring. Ring. Ring. Ring. Click. "Hi, there! Yancey's real sorry she can't come to the phone right now but do leave your dimensions and she'll get back to you A. S. A. P. Truly. So speak your piece right after the beep. Beep."

Wanda Lou looked with disgust at the enemy telephone. "Yancey, there are times I could kill you. Oh, no. Mustn't say that. I know you're hiding out at home and screening your calls but enough already. There has been a terrible—well, I guess you could call it a disaster. Get back to me. Please. PLEASE."

Double damn. Yancey wasn't acting like herself ever since she took up with that Clovis who says he's not interested in being an actor. Bull. Just playing hard to get. Everybody wants to be an actor. Actors! All the traits of a dog except loyalty. This new catastrophe would certainly put a lot of talents to the test. She looked at the blank television screen in the armoir to her right and shuddered as she flashed back on the last image. A closeup of a number-three knitting needle protruding from Wally's neck. Her first reaction had been that it was another one of Wally's tasteless jokes. A way of provoking what people really thought about Mr. Producer Waldemar Krog. But then the image had frozen and gone slowly to black. It became quite real as the whole building seemed to rumble. A whispered gasp that grew louder and louder as everyone emerged from offices and production rooms, gathering to verify what they had seen.

"Why must Wanda Lou always push the panic button?" Nude Yancey asked nude Clovis lying beside her on the flower-patterned Porthault sheets of her king-sized bed.

"If you didn't keep the volume all the way up on that infernal machine, you wouldn't hear every call. You could blissfully ignore the world until you were in a mood to cope."

"Smart ass. And it is," as she gave him a loving tap. "How did I get so lucky?" She ran her index finger from the top of his forehead slowly down the center of his nose to his lips and paused to allow him to purse his lips in the semblance of a kiss.

"Luck? Fate's more like it. Go call your friend. Third call's the charmer. And, I have no desire to play a thousand questions about why Wanda Lou called when you can get it from her directly."

"But she cries wolf so often and maybe she's just . . ."

"No discussion. Call her."

Yancey slid off the bed. "Stop looking at me like that. I won't have the strength to lift the receiver." Clovis grinned, acknowledging her soft white curves as she covered them with a white terry robe.

"Okay, Wanda Lou, this better be good." She dialed. "Busy. I should have known. Typical. Call me please and then she gets on the phone." She pressed the redial on her phone. Again and again. Then she tried the front desk, the Make-Up room, the Actors' Lounge, Wardrobe, the Hair Room, the Control Room, the Prop Room and Tracy George's dressing room because she had her own phone installed. And the Scene Dock, the Audio Room, the Video Room and editing. Finally, in desperation she tried the Writers' Office and then Allie Jones and Marti Liverski's offices at United Broadcasting System's Headquarters. All were busy. Exasperated, she turned to Clovis who had since showered and dressed. "This catastrophe must be something to write—or I should say—call home about. And, if Wanda Lou had been trying to get me again,

I've got that Call Waiting gimmick. Something tells me to go to the Studio."

"And something tells me to go with you."

At the time, it seemed the most natural approach to the situation. In retrospect, no one could believe it. Least of all Chuck Rosen, the Director. As soon as the body was discovered, Chuck took charge. And directed.

Chuck ordered Arnie Steloff, the Technical Director, to do a freeze-frame of Wally with the Quantel (the name of which he could never remember before or since), and then to kill the feed from Camera Two. He commanded Props to rope off the Sheraton Library, making it a hot set. He dispatched Trudy von Richter, the Associate Director, to inform Security and make sure that no one left or entered the building. He had Joey Savage, the Stage Manager, call the Police. He asked Nickie Pastori, the Production Assistant, to deal with Johnny Krog. He suggested to Maud Sterling, character actress, that she would be the ideal person to comfort Jolie Dornya in the Hair Room. And, with a final surge of adrenalin, Chuck commandeered Maxwell Arden, the senior member of the cast, to get Allie Jones to come to the Studio floor immediately. This was her problem, not his. Then he collapsed in the huge brown leather winged chair in the Lansing Living Room set up directly across from the Sheraton Library. Looking at Wally's body, he suddenly realized that the son-of-a-bitch was really dead. He lowered his head, hoping that no one had seen the huge grin on his face.

Before going up to Wally's office where a long story meeting was taking place, Maxwell Arden went to his dressing room to check out how he looked. Somehow it was fitting that he had been chosen to deliver the news of Wally's death to the writers and executives gathered for the purpose of creating exciting future stories for THE KEY TO LIFE. After all, he had played Dwight Edgerton, the richest man in Clearview, U.S.A., from the first day the show went on the air fifteen years ago. The Scion of the Clan. The edges between Maxwell and Dwight had become blurred through the years. They spoke as one.

As he gave his very full pompadour of white hair a final tap, he could hear Wally's mocking voice: "You are a very lucky man that you have your hair. Go bald and you could not get a job. You are not an actor. You are a mannequin with a full head of real hair." It had become more and more difficult not to answer his taunts. There had been producers before and there would be producers after Wally Krog. The show would go on and on as long as the Maxwell Arden Fan Clubs existed and he received hundreds of adoring letters every week. He knew a great deal about Fan Clubs and viewers and how popularity was gauged. He had become an expert on this phase of the business. It paid off in bread and butter and alimony.

It had never occurred to Maxwell to become an actor until it had been thrust upon him by being in the right place (Hollywood) at the right time (1942). He went from pumping gas to pumping iron when patriotic actors were going off to war. Because of faulty vision, Maxwell was drafted to be an actor and play at being a soldier. The forever best friend who didn't get the girl, he became the Grade B movie prince. Never a king. Reliable, punctual, lines down pat, as his hair went from black to gray, Maxwell went from juvenile to character actor and fewer and fewer roles. First he had his eyes done and then a little tuck around the jaw line. The only tuck that counted was the one in his bank account. Tall, distinguished, with a somewhat familiar name, he was rescued from oblivion by the once despised art form —the soap opera. The comfortable, lucrative home for big-screen rejects.

Maxwell rehearsed his speech to Allie and the writers in the mirror. Satisfied, he left his dressing room, locking the door behind him. Oblivious to the clusters of shocked faces in the hall, he made his way to Wally's office, cleared his throat a few times and then knocked bruskly on the door before opening it. All faces turned toward him as he closed the door.

"I know this is most irregular," he began with an apology for his intrusion, "but there has been a tragedy." Pausing for emphasis, he made eye contact with each one around the table. Tillie, Dewey, Nora, Allie and Marti. All of them seemed puzzled. Indicating the blank screens of the television sets in the office, "If the set with the feed from the control room had been on, you would have known."

Pompous old bore, thought Tillie. She said, "Please come to the point, Max." She always had to catch herself from calling him by his character name.

"It's at times like this, dear Tillie, that I wish I had a script because I know you could say this better than I. I've been asked to tell you that Wally is not with us anymore."

"What do you mean?" Dewey challenged. "He was here just a few minutes ago before we took our break."

"He went out for a smoke," Nora explained.

"But he didn't return when we did. He was gone so long Allie sent Johnny to look for him." Marti adding her proverbial two cents.

"What is it, Max?" Allie asked, like a mother addressing a three-year-old.

"Wally is dead," Maxwell said as simply as he could, watching the changes of expression on each face. "It was on the television but you didn't have it on."

"Oh, my God," Allie said in almost a whisper, covering her mouth with her hand. "But everyone else in the building has seen . . ."

"And don't forget the feed also goes to UBS," Marti reminded her.

"What? How?" Tillie asked. "Max, for once in your life talk faster!"

"He was murdered in the Sheraton Library. And, Allie, Chuck wants you to meet him there on the Studio floor." And giving Tillie a scornful look, he turned on his heel. Literally.

"Wait, Max," said Tillie, going after him. "I didn't mean to snap at you. It's a classic example of blaming the messenger for the message. Truly, Max. Will you forgive me?" She reached out her hand.

Max took her hand and brushed his lips on it, murmuring, "I already have."

Allie pushed past the whispering groups and headed down the stairs for the Studio. Obviously Patrick hadn't seen whatever it was everyone saw or he would have tracked her down. She had to find out the facts before speaking to him. There was no way in the world that the news could be contained. Every office and room had a television set which could pick up the Control Room feed when turned to channel six. This would be the one morning when everyone watched blocking instead of favorite shows on other channels. The instant communicator had done its work well. Every telephone in the building was broadcasting to the outside world the miracle of Waldemar Krog's demise. And each call would prompt another in an endless chain. Was there anyone who would truly mourn him? As she hurried by the closed door of the Hair Room, she heard sobs. She was tempted to go in but thought better of it. Do not let yourself get distracted. Don't flit about. Concentrate.

Opening the heavy studio door, Allie paused to get her bearings. The Sheraton Library was always at the far end on the right. It was the one permanent set, because it was impractical to take down and put up thanks to its magnificent, curved stairway. There was an unnatural hush. The stage hands were standing in groups and not in their usual lounge positions on the furniture of the various sets. Clasping and unclasping her hands, she forced herself toward the white blur of Wally's hair. In her rush, she had forgotten her eyeglasses. Someone touched her arm and she jumped.

Her head made little palsied, bird like darts until she focused. "Oh, Chuck, it's you," she whispered. "Max told us. Have the Police been called?"

"Yes," said Chuck, guiding her by her elbow to a table at the Blueprint Cafe. "I'll tell you everything I've put in motion. But you don't have to whisper. None of us have to whisper anymore."

Well, here I go again, thought Maud Sterling as she left the Studio and headed for the Hair Room. Wally Krog might turn out to be as much trouble dead as he had been alive. Everything that man came in contact with was slanted for disaster. From falling ratings to fraught women. There was hardly a soul in the Studio who did not know that Wally was sleeping with Jolie. Such a euphemism. With Wally, even "fucking" would be an exaggeration. "Banging," yes, that was the word for Wally's rabbit exercises.

When Maud entered the Hair Room, it seemed completely empty. Then she noticed a spiral of smoke coming from the corner beyond the dirty towels. A crumpled Jolie was seated on the floor, knees to chest, a cigarette dangling from her mouth. She stared at Maud and then in a child like voice asked, "Is it true?"

"Yes," answered Maud. And that's when the howling began.

"Please, Jolie, get off the floor. Come on darling," said Maud as she tugged her to her feet and maneuvered her into one of the barber chairs. "Sshh, Sshh," she crooned, attempting to cradle Jolie's head against her firm bosom, even though she was aware that the tears might stain her one-of-a-kind pink silk blouse.

Jolie suddenly pushed her away and growled at the door, "What are you staring at, you freak!"

Maud turned to see Jeff Landon swaying in the door, flask in hand.

"I only thought," he mumbled, with an offering gesture.

"Jeff, knock off the stuff. We all have a long day ahead of us.

Get some coffee," Maud advised as she shut the door in his face. A loud wail. "Volume does not necessarily express grief, Jolie. For your sake, for *his* sake get a grip on yourself." Snuffles. "We will all have a lot of questions to answer." Blubbering, followed by a hiccup. Maud filled a paper cup with water, pryed the cigarette from the corner of Jolie's mouth, and made her take a few sips. Yes, a lot of questions. How far back would they go? "That's a good girl." Good? Bad? What were the barometers. She once had a good girl. Or was she bad? So very long ago or was it yesterday? She started to wonder about Jolie's mother. How little they all knew each other, they who worked together so intimately every day. Complete little cells without encumberments. Total units with no attachments. Here a wife, there a child but other than an occasional soon forgotten introduction, who belonged to what or to whom. "Murder cracked open lives like a walnut." It sort of went like that, the half-remembered speech from CHALK GARDEN in which she had played at the beginning. So many beginnings. She suddenly became aware that Jolie had quieted down and was staring at her.

"Thank you, Maud," she said quietly. "It was the shock. You see, only last week, he said he would marry me. He would leave his wife . . . and marry me."

"And you believed him." It was a statement not a question.

"Yes, because I wanted to. I knew he never would. But, I hoped."

"And where there's life there's hope." I can't believe I said anything that banal, thought Maud, as Jolie nodded.

A gentle knock preceded the slow opening of the door to reveal a tall, handsome white-haired woman swathed in electric blue leather. "May I?" she asked looking from Maud to Jolie.

"Victoria?" said a surprised Maud. "Vickie! What on earth are you doing here?"

"Jolie was going to give my hair a trim on the lunch break today." The voice was hoarse, husky, whispery, cigarette cultivated. "I was early so when I bumped into Maggie, I shmoozed with her in her dressing room And then I heard. Oh, my poor Jolie," she said preempting Maud's place beside the suffering Jolie. Another tearfall started. "There, there." Maud made eye contact with Vicky and raised her delicately penciled eyebrows, Vicky raised her heavy grey eyebrows. They had communicated the whole tragic story.

The "five" was now a full hour. No one could leave the building.

"But, officer, I always go home now to walk my dog. I just live two blocks away and—"

"Sorry, lady," said the ruddy faced policewoman who seemed to be guarding the front door of the Studio. "No one is to leave the building."

"Please," begged Maggie List, "I'll be back in five minutes. Penny will be so upset. I don't know what she'll do."

"Well, I guess you're going to find out. Sorry. Nobody leaves. Orders. Police orders."

Broken lunch dates. Bicycled Chinese food. Greek salads in foil and plastic. Mustard-heavy deli rye sandwiches. Pizzas with and without anchovies. And all television sets tuned to Channel 8 to watch today's air show of KEY. It saved conversation. It saved having to take a pro or con stand on Wally Krog. It saved exchanges of where were you when.

The UBS switchboard deflected all incoming calls. The body was taken out the back of the Studio through the Scene Dock where the sets were brought in and out. With Detective Herbert Kaufman in charge, everything was on hold. A short pigeon-chested man who walked like a penguin, he was determined not to be impressed with all these stars, these show folk (as he thought of them). After patrolling the halls, he decided to take decisive action and asked Chuck (who seemed to him to be the leader) to make an announcement.

"Attention! Attention!" For once the public address system

could be heard throughout the building. "Everyone in the building is to come to the Studio. Everyone! Actors, crew, support people, engineers, production staff, visitors, editors, cleaning people, stage hands. And you guys on the lighting grid, full lights in the Studio and then hightail it down here. Everyone please come to the Studio. Now. Not later. NOW!"

Clearly, Herbert Kaufman was not expecting to see over two hundred people arrive in the Studio. He looked up at Chuck who towered over him, "Do all these people have work here?"

"Yes. With one or two exceptions they all have jobs that get done so we can do our little hour-a-day show." Another asshole, thought Chuck, who thinks the actors make up their own words in real living rooms.

"Jeeesus." Wait til the wife hears this. That lady in the pink blouse whose hair seemed to be tilting looked familiar. Lydia. Yeah that was it. Lydia, his wife's favorite. Every night she would tell him how Lydia whupped all the guys in town.

"Detective Kaufman," it was the bird lady with the big eyeglasses, "if you don't mind, I think I should address these people before you do. You see, I'm Vice-President of Daytime Programming and I would like to explain our plans for today's show."

"Show must go on." Herbert was right on top of things.

"Quiet please, I have something to say," said Allie clapping her hands.

"Shut the hell up!" roared Chuck and everyone did. "Here, Allie," and Chuck helped her climb on a coffee table in the Lansing Living Room.

"Thank you. I would like to thank you all for being so cooperative. Obviously, we cannot continue today's show. I do not wish to minimize the tragedy but I must also be practical. The show that you were to do today will be split over several days or done on a Saturday. We have to work that out. However, tomorrow's show will be done as scheduled. Unfortunately, we are only three days ahead of air with shows in the can and cannot take time off.

I have spoken to Patrick who agrees with this. Now I'll turn you over to Detective Kaufman." She started to get off the table and stopped. "Just a word of caution. Please do not discuss what happened here today with members of the Press. We are working on a formal announcement and I'll see that you all will get copies of it." Chuck helped her off the table. She thought she had spotted Victoria Jessup at the edge of the crowd and headed in that direction. "Victoria, I can't believe you're here. When you're through, please come see me in Nora Easton's office. Vickie, you're an answer to a prayer, an answer to a prayer."

"Okay, folks, we're going to take your name, address and what you do here. You, Director, set it up."

Nobody spoke to Chuck Rosen like that. Nobody. Chuck looked down at the small, strutting man and resisted the urge to give him a famous Rosen direction on spectacular ways to use his anatomy. Eyes closed, gritted teeth, he sighed. "Okay," he started, noticing the smiles of those who knew what an effort this was causing him. "Okay. Actors first, then Engineers, then Support and so on. Hell, you guys know the pecking order."

Arnie Steloff put his fist in Chuck's face. "Engineers supposed to go first."

"Not now, Arnie, I'm too beat," said Chuck. Arnie noticed that he did look grayer than usual and gave him a great hug. "Thanks." Chuck then headed for the Cafe set which had been turned into a makeshift police headquarters.

"Hey, Riley," Clovis greeted the police woman on guard at the entrance of the Studio. "Still keeping the department honest?"

"Well, if it ain't Kelley himself," she answered, turning another shade more red, "What're you doing here? I thought you was out in California becoming a big star."

"Hell, I didn't have to go to California for that. Here, meet a real star, Yancey Howland. Rebecca Riley."

"You're Sally," said Riley, even redder.

"How nice to meet a fan," smiled Yancey. "But when do you get to watch our show?"

"Tape. Greatest thing ever happened. Set it up for a week at a time. And every night as soon as I get home I have THE KEY TO LIFE."

"What's happening. Why all the Blue turnout?"

"Some guy got killed." Clovis put his arm around Yancey to steady her. "Not one of the actors. Had a funny name like Crag or Glog. He was murdered on the Sheraton Library set."

"Krog?" asked Yancey tentatively.

"Yeah, that's him. I think he was a producer or something."

Yancey sagged against Clovis. "Thank God, you're my alibi."

"Hey, Kelley, you're going to love this." Riley grinned as she turned off her walkie-talkie. "Guess who's running the operation?" She scrunched her neck down and her shoulders up and started to walk stiffly with her arm chopping the air.

"Napoleon? Riley, I know it's against the rules but you've got to let me in there to see him in action."

"Seeing as how it's you," Riley nodded and as Clovis bent down to place a kiss on her cheek, she achieved high magenta.

The more Allie tried to keep her voice under control, the more it quivered. At least she was able to keep it in a low register and out of the screechy highs that took over when she became agitated. Her hands were so unsteady, she could not coordinate her usual hairpin swirl. She stared unseeingly out the window of Nora Easton's office.

"Patrick, I am listening. And I thank you for your confidence. Now do me the courtesy of hearing what I have to say. That man, that Herbert Kaufman, detective, has done more to destroy the morale of the KEY company in one hour than Wally Krog did in six months. He does not know how to handle anybody, including himself. I don't care if you have to call the Mayor or the Governor or the President, he must be replaced. At once. UBS has too much

invested financially and we all have too much invested emotionally to let that stupid, vulgar, arrogant, ridiculous, incompetent—
yes, Patrick. Marti is working on the Press Release. I'll stay at this
extension until I hear from you. Thank you." Allie hung up and
swivelled away from the window.

The daytime serials's never ending treadmill. For five days a
week, from Monday through Friday, a new show with no repeats.
Holidays were only possible by working on Saturdays. At times,
she almost prayed for a natural disaster so that the shows would
be pre-empted—anything: a market crash, a freak snowfall, an
airplane explosion, a child in a well. No. *No.* Nothing that serious.
Maybe an attempted assassination so that UPS News would take
over for an hour or even two and some of the shows could get
ahead. Like the Iran-Contra hearings. A true blessing. Sans blood.
The fans always called up and complained but that made them
even more eager for the next episodes.

And now they were another show behind. But, it was possible
that the tasteful publicity that would grow rancid in the tabloids
might snare a few curious viewers. With the ratings slipping,
Wally had picked a good day to be murdered.

# Chapter 3

Before rigor mortis stiffened Wally Krog's body, Victoria Jessup gallantly agreed to produce KEY once again. Yes, she was able to start immediately since the many projects she had in development were pending. She was indeed sure that an equitable deal could be worked out between her lawyer and UBS Business Affairs. She humbly received Allie's peck on the cheek and "save the day/answer to a prayer/stroke of luck" and other like clichés. She knew very well that the bottom line was that the damned show *did* have to go on and there was not another soul available at that very moment. Anyway, not one who knew the show's workings and people intimately. Certainly, none of Wally's acolytes was capable.

Victoria freely admitted that she was superstitious. She would use that small, spare windowless room behind the rehearsal hall. No, it was definite, she would not use Wally's office. True, it had been hers before it was his, but she was convinced that a fault lay somewhere in the panelled walls. Obviously, the Great Soap Opera God Herself had put a curse on that office.

If that's what she wants to believe, thought Clovis, that was fine with him. That office would be an ideal place for him to become absorbed into the KEY company. He could interview the hundreds involved without disrupting the show's production and could observe its mechanics without being intrusive. It would be interesting to note how various people reacted to this spare, ugly room with its four television sets and giant cork bulletin board.

Over two hundred suspects, three entrances, two floors plus a roof and grid. No locked-room mystery this. The knitting needle, ultimate death instrument, had belonged to one of the actresses. It was doubtful that anyone came in off the street at the right second to kill Wally and left without being seen. It would have to be someone working on KEY, or at least connected to someone working on it. For even if the killer was not working that day, like Yancey, his/her presence would not be noted as unusual. As Clovis soon discovered, signing in and out at the guard's desk at the front of the Studio was only done by an unknown who needed help. The back door and Scene Dock were not patrolled in any way. Security was a lost art on the East Coast.

As soon as it was established that Clovis Kelley would be responsible for solving the Krog murder, Nora Easton attached herself to him. A thin prim woman with a quick little nervous smile that clocked on and off at computed intervals. Nora Easton, Mrs. Eugene (Bud) Easton, Associate Producer. She'd been with the show three years and knew everything and everyone. She had the office right next to his. And if there was anything, *anything* he wanted or needed, she would be more than happy to arrange it for him. Schedules, scripts, outlines, crew and actor lists, paper, pens, calendars, Xeroxes—just name it. Nothing would be too big or too small for her to do. Yes, it was true that Vickie—Victoria Jessup—needed her services. As did Hair, Make Up, Wardrobe and Publicity but she did believe that solving poor Wally's death took top priority. What could she do?

What she could do, he thought, was to shut up. When he said he would start with coffee, she was ready to fly and get it for him. No, he could get it himself. He knew his way to the Actors' Lounge where he had been a few times with Yancey. However, he would be most grateful if she would get him the names, addresses and functions of those working on KEY. Or, anything else she thought important.

By the time Clovis got back to the office with coffee, the oval table was stacked high with neat piles of paper. Nora surveyed her handiwork like an eager puppy waiting to be patted. She informed him that contracts and long story lines could be found in the file drawers hidden in the long, low cabinet that covered the width of the room. No, as far as she knew no one had been in the office since yesterday's aborted meeting.

Alone at last, Clovis sighed. That lady sure had a need to be needed. He didn't envy her husband. He started to examine some of the grouping of papers on the table. Seventh Revision on one, Tenth Revision on another. Trees died for this. Before drowning in the pool of paper, he took the list from his inner pocket that had been put together by the police yesterday. By seven last evening, little Napoleon Kaufman had willingly turned it over to him with one of his pompous speeches on procedure. He also proudly showed Lydia's signed eight-by-ten glossy: "To Ceil Kaufman, with best wishes from your friend Maud Sterling (Lydia)."

He would have to restructure yesterday to know where each person on that list had been at the approximate time of death— 11:15 A.M. And, of course, the motive. Just because Wally was hated by almost everyone on the show, it was not reason enough to kill him. It could also be something closer to home, having nothing to do with the show. Certainly his office held no profile of the man. Except for a few miniature tin soldiers glaring at each other in mock combat atop the cabinet, there was nothing of a personal nature. Strange that there was not even a phone book or wheeldex or engagement calendar. Had someone removed them? A coffee mug imprinted with a heart with an "I" before and a "Soaps" after held a few sharpened #2 Eberhard Fabers and thick green pentels. One desk drawer was crammed with paper napkins, straws, soy sauce in plasticine, sugar packets and a collection of plastic forks and spoons. Another had an assortment of various size pads. Had Mr. Krog guarded himself so carefully out of fantasy or fear?

Clovis played back that very first meeting with Wally when he had insisted on showing off his domain. During the tour, Wally had introduced Clovis to no one nor had he acknowledged the occasional "Hi" or smile. "You and I are very much alike. Men of the world. That is why we understand each other. Sometimes I wonder how these people (a disdainful sweep of the hand encompassing everyone working in the Studio) manage to function in life. They have so little imagination, so little appreciation. The fool woman who was here before me, Victoria Jessup? You do not know her? Lucky for you. Typical. She used to say she was the 'Mayor of Clearview.' What a small mind. At least she could have thought herself President or Queen. As for me, I may settle for King. Yes, King. For all this is mine and I say what does and does not happen. I have the right to make anything I wish happen."

Your basic pulling-wings-off-flies man, thought Clovis. His favorite ploy was to threaten to exile someone from KEY and then banish that person from Soap Land forever. And now the king was dead. Long live the conveniently on-the-spot Mayor?

Marti Livorski opened the door to her "E" apartment on the 31st floor of the Tower Apartments and peered furtively down the elegant papered (with matching blue carpet) blue hall. No one in sight. She pressed the button on the side of the door to allow for a quick reentry and then moved stealthily down to the "B" apartment and opened the door with the key she had clenched in her fist. It was the apartment she had found for Wally six months ago. So convenient to the Studio. So convenient for her to keep an eye on him.

Closing the door behind her, she voiced a timid "Hello?". Just playing it safe. No answer. The living room of the apartment had a magnificent view of the Jersey shore, all the way from Weehawken to the George Washington Bridge. The apartment was so high up that there was no need for curtains to keep the world from peeking. The cotton white levelors that matched the walls were only for escaping some of the more eye-shattering sunsets. The furniture that had been called Swedish Modern in its Forties popularity peak, now seemed merely uncomfortable and old fashioned. The only ultra-modern touch was a teakwood unit that sported a 24-inch TV and enough stereo equipment and VCRs for a small theatre. All, of course, paid for by UBS and installed by UBS engineers. A producer must have equipment at home.

He had plenty of equipment, all right, thought Marti as she crossed left to the scene of her seduction: the bedroom with its King-size bed. Fit for a King! In replaying their first sexual encounter, she wasn't quite sure who had been the seducer. Her pride, her heavy Jewish breasts, had drawn him to his knees. Too bad about Wally. She would miss planning those little soirées when Lincoln Livorsky was visiting mills in the South or on trips to Hong Kong and Paris. Her excuse for no longer accompanying him was a simple one—work. She smiled wistfully, with such work she didn't need vacations. She gave the bed a little goodbye pat and started to examine the closet and wardrobe to make sure there was no evidence of her liasons dangereuses.

The closet had his few dark blue suits and many pairs of jeans in various shades of fade. An unimportant group of ties limply hung on a hanger. Two identical bathrobes of one-size-fits-all navy-blue velour. One for him and one for her. Whoever the her happened to be. She flipped through his laundry-returned cardboarded checked shirts (Large—16) in every possible color combination. The socks were all black. Calvin Klein shorts were in a neat grouping. She started to flush as she remembered sliding her hand into the fold and felt his growing response.

The sound of a key opening the front door quickly erased her erotic reverie. Softly closing the drawer, she sidled into the living room. It was Johnny Krog carrying a Vuitton two-suiter that had seen a brighter past.

"Moving in?" Marti asked.

"No, my mother asked me to pick out the clothes to bury my father."

For the first time, she noticed how strongly he resembled Wally. The same Steve Canyon jaw, stubby nose and fleshy lips. When his thick, wavy dark hair turned white, he would look exactly like a slender edition of his father. "Wally had borrowed some tapes that we need desperately but I can't find them anywhere," she smoothly explained her presence. "Need any help?" she volunteered.

"I don't think so."

"Are you okay?" she asked. His face had no expression, his voice was low. Whenever anyone asked Wally if he had children, he always answered that he had two-and-a-half boys. The half referred to Johnny, his youngest. He would then explain that his estranged wife, Elizabeth, had turned the boy into a sissy, a pansy.

Johnny seemed to think about her question and then answered, "I'm okay. We never did get along. I'm sorry he had to go like that. But we all have to go sometimes." And he walked into the bedroom.

The Writers' Office was not at the Studio. The writers liked this separation, since the actors could not always ask them about story lines and or suggest ridiculous plots for their characters. Each actor seemed to believe that he/she was the only one on the show.

The Office was within walking distance of the Studio in a rundown ex-factory one-elevator push-button building. It was remarkable only for the size of its roaches, which Tillie Ryan said she preferred to the actors. The few dark rooms were furnished in UBS-issue discarded green metal and scarred wood desks. No one made any attempt to fix it up because it gave the writers reason for working at home. Except for morning conferences, only the switchboard/typist (who never stayed for more than a few weeks), actually worked there. Dewey's office was distinguished by a few framed pictures of the wife and the children. When Tillie was there, she used the round table in the conference room. A broken yellow Venetian blind, metal folding chairs, water cooler and a Mr. Coffee completed the decor. The toilet was in the dimly lit hall.

Elbows on table, Tillie was having an animated telephone talk with Allie. "Yes, yes. I understand. He's here now," she said as Dewey walked in and she signaled him to sit down. "I'll explain it to him. Thank you, Allie." Batting her mascared lashes at him, she broke into a huge smile. "She's afraid I'll go over her head to Patrick."

"And what were you going to explain to me?"

"That." she said pointing to the newspaper in his hand. He tossed the last edition of the New York Post on the table facing her. DEATH IN THE AFTERNOON. "Allie was saying that the Press got the information before UBS had a chance to do a release. One of those mysterious leaks."

"Leaks! Leaks!" Dewey spat out petulantly. "I'll bet you even money that Allie herself called her friend—what's her name—?"

"Liz Smith," Tillie told him. "But she's at the News. At least it's a respectable quote. Frankly, I was expecting much worse. And that's a good picture of Wally fawning over our so-called "Star". Turn to page three, it says. Ah, an obvious play on words: 'Would the Key to Life Unlock the Door to Death'."

"So much for dignity," he said, looking martyred.

"What did you expect, Dewey. Get real. We live in a goldfish bowl and when something juicy like a murder happens, it's big news. Also, it will sell tickets. And yesterday you were worrying about starving to death. Get me some coffee."

The corners of his mouth were so far down, he looked strangely like a hound. "I don't know how you can take this—this—this experience so lightly," he said as he went to the coffee machine.

"I'm not taking it lightly, Dewey, I'm only putting it in perspective. Wally is dead. I'm sorry. But there is nothing I can do about it." He's in one of those why-am-I-wasting-my-talent moods that Tillie recognized so well. Their relationship slid from collaborators to mother/son. And he was useful even if he did not have a creative bone in that rangey body. "This too shall pass."

Dewey dutifully poured the contents of two saccharine packets into the styrofoam cup, stirred it and handed it to Tillie. "Easy enough for you to say," he mumbled. "Every Tom, Dick and Harry has been on the phone to me this morning wanting to know the *real* story. How am I supposed to get any work done?"

Tillie stood up and smoothed the tight grey and yellow striped dress over her thin hips. "Now, Dewey, you're not the only one being used. Just ignore them. Tell DeeDee to say you're at the office and then tell—what's her name this week—to say you're home." She walked to him and, putting her hands on his shoulders, she looked into his mournful dark eyes. "There's a lot of work for all of us to do without your creating more by bitching."

"What do you know about this genius Kelley they've hired to solve this whole mess?" he asked.

"He used to be with the Police Department in Homicide before he quit and went to the Coast to be a consultant on every cop show you've seen in the last five years. The Police Department has reinstated him because he has the advantage of knowing a lot about 'show biz' and also about KEY. He's Yancey's latest," she smiled, "and very attractive."

"Swell. That's just what we need. Another Yancey 'fella.' Didn't the last one run the gallery where we rented our props until they caught him over-charging? Yancey Howland's taste in men is about as great as her acting ability."

"Dewey! As Wally's death has proven, no one is indispensable. In our very small and redundant world of Daytime, we are a very select few. A specialized group dancing around musical chairs and switching loyalties with each different tune. We are a unique and exclusive clique. And do not forget for one tiny second that *I* hold the key to life in more ways than one. I have made excuses for your little tantrums in the past because I kept hoping that your attitudes would change. Frankly, dear Dewey, I'm reaching the point where I don't give a fucking damn." She then walked out of the room and slammed the door.

Dewey slumped into a chair, holding his breath in an attempt not to hyperventilate. Steady, he told himself, steady.

The front desk telephone answerer and people deflector at THE KEY TO LIFE was named Barbie Dixon. She had gotten the job because her father's law partner's wife's mother belonged to the same bridge club as Patrick's secretary's aunt. After barely squeaking through Riverdale High, she reached nirvana at nineteen since she had been a fan of KEY for eleven years. The only information that her brain absorbed was clued to KEY and she could recite facts, figures and plot intricacies with computer accuracy. And, as an avid reader of SOAP OPERA DIGEST and all other magazines devoted to Daytime Drama, she also felt she knew the lives of the Stars intimately. She was the ultimate buff.

Barbie had loved Wally but thought that Clovis Kelley was much better looking. She was anxiously waiting for a break in his busy, busy day so she could tell him some of the story lines he had asked about.

"Hello, Key to Life. I'm sorry, ma'am, you'll just have to watch the show. I am not allowed to tell you whether Sam and Gray are going to get together. Thank you." Her round chipmunk cheeks glowed with the pleasure of power. "Hello, Key to Life. Oh, Milo. Your call tomorrow is at seven-thirty. No cuts yet. Yes, it's a little quiet here today. See you tomorrow."

Barbie felt someone behind her and two rough hands covered her eyes. She knew by the smell. "Cut it out, Jeff."

"The door is closed. Does Kelley have someone in there with him?"

"No, but," she pointed to a lighted button on her telephone, "he's talking to someone."

"Who?"

"He made the call himself. You know you shouldn't ask."

Jeff leaned over and kissed her forehead. "But you'd tell Uncle Jeff, wouldn't you?"

"You're terrible." she giggled. "Hello, Key to Life. Mrs. Krog? Yes, Mr. Kelley is here but he's on the phone right now. I'll have him get back to you. Yes, I have the number."

"Let me get in there, first." Jeff pleaded. "I really have to talk to him."

Barbie shrugged and they both stared at the lit button.

Clovis had dialed Yancey. She had pounced on her beige desk phone on the first ring. "Hello!"

"Well, hello to you, too," said a surprised Clovis. "Where's the famous 'Hi'?"

"Oh, darling, I'm so glad it's you," she exclaimed.

"And I'm glad it's you and I don't have to read my prepared machine speech."

"Clovis, you know the way I have my machine set to pick up after the fourth ring? And, if I'm at home and not otherwise occupied, I pick up on the third ring. Well, in the last half hour I've had three hangups after I said Hi."

"A lot of heavy breathing?"

"Be serious. It was spooky. The first time I thought it was the wrong number. And even the second time. But three times? Anyway, it is so good to hear your breathing. I wish I could feel it," she added, allowing her voice to dip into sultry. "Do you realize it's almost twenty four hours since I've seen you. I'm having withdrawal symptoms."

"I think Dr. Kelley can cure those," smiled Clovis. She sure knew how to bring out the adolescent in him. "I'm told that out time today is supposed to be seven. But with Vickie's first-day jitters and everyone else's post-murder confusions, I don't think they'll finish taping that early."

"My, you sure picked up the lingo fast. But then I've known for quite a while you're a speedy learner. Want me to pick you up at eight or would you prefer avoiding that?"

"No, babe, let's give them a show. One less thing for the folk to speculate. Right?" He liked this woman. A lot.

"You've come a long way, baby," she crooned. "See you eightish. Consider yourself kissed." She made kissing sounds and Clovis found himself almost doing the same thing. Was it her honesty, her sweetness, her humor or her innocence that had gotten to him? Innocence? Yes, like the legendary Esmerelda, Yancey had the ability to be a virgin with each new lover.

The moment he put the phone down, there was a knock and the door opened. Jeff Landon stood on the threshold. "Please, can I see you now?" he asked urgently.

"Sure," said Clovis rising to shake hands with him. "You're Jeff Landon. Sit down."

"Yeah. Technically I'm Jeff R. Landon, which distinguishes me from another Jeff Landon I've never seen but his membership in the union, AFTRA and I guess also SAG and AEA, is before me. So the 'R' makes us different. Anyway that's not what I came to see you about. Yeah." He adjusted the collar of his Polo wool plaid shirt. "Sorry to barge in like this but they don't need me again until the sixth act and I had some free time." He rubbed his unshaven chin a few times. "I don't shave until before air. I don't go for that 'Miami Vice' look."

"Well, what did you want to see me about?" Clovis prodded, leaning back in his chair and crossing his ankles under the table. Relaxed pose number one, which puts the other party at ease.

"I wanted to tell you before anyone else did it for me. Yeah. I hated that son-of-a-bitch Wally Krog. And I'm not sorry he's dead. But I didn't kill him. Too squeamish." Clovis smiled and then Jeff smiled. "Joke."

"From what I gather, Jeff," first names in this business, "you're not alone in your attitude. Was there a specific reason that you weren't fond of him?"

"Fond." Jeff rubbed the index finger of his right hand back and forth across his thick reddish brown moustache. "I never heard of the bastard before he took over this show six months ago. I've been on the show, let me see, four, maybe five years. So we had a new producer. Big deal. This is my third soap and I've been through a lot of kooks. Yeah. Anyway, I've got this open mind about him. Ask anyone, I mind my own business. Don't quote me but this family shit that goes on around here ain't for me. Sure I do softball sometimes when we play another show but I don't hang out. Anyway, Wally-boy arrives and starts to set up his gang. The Macho Boys. Some of the camera guys, Frank, Lester, a few of the actors like Gary and Ray. They go to that dumb Y and do machines or go for drinks after the show with lots of tits and ass talk. He never wanted to go home so he'd find excuses to do scenes over and over. And then he'd laugh if some of us got pissed off because we had better things to do." He paused abruptly and then said in a heavy accent, "If you want to get out early tonight, get me a woman."

"You could scare a lot of people with that imitation." Clovis smiled.

"Thanks. God knows I heard him enough. Yeah. So anyway, I don't know what started him but he took a special pleasure in trying to get my goat. You know, there are guys like that. They need one person to pick on, then they gather their cronies and laugh about him. I was it. Right on the fucking bull's eye. I wasn't alone, by the way, there were a few others. He'd test, put the knife in—and then twist. Yeah. He started a rumor about me. I've got this agent, Damon Mandel. There's no such thing as a good agent but as agents go, Damon did all right by me. He only handles me for daytime not for commercials or films. Yeah." He hooked his hands together and looked down at them. Silence.

Clovis watched Jeff try to talk. It was very difficult for him and he muttered a few "yeahs" under his breath. Decision. He looked up and faced Clovis. "Damon's got AIDS. He's got the spots, the grey look, the works. Another couple of weeks, maybe a month or two. Anyway, Wally suggests that I've got AIDS. Bastard! You don't get it shaking hands and I've never been closer to Damon than that. First insinuations, then remarks. Believe me, I would have taken a blood test but I didn't want to give that slime the satisfaction that he'd affected me. So I ignored the whole bit until a few weeks ago when our "Star" refuses to kiss me."

Fists clenched, Jeff stood up and started to pace. "I'm clean. I'm clean."

"How did you resolve that one?" Clovis asked.

Jeff threw his head back and roared with laughter. "I told the bitch that I'd get a blood test if she would. After all, how the hell do I know what that husband of hers is doing when he's not servicing her. And there have been stories. Yeah. So then it all faded away, But I wanted to tell you about it before anyone else got to you. Thanks for listening." He held out his hand and Clovis shook it. "My greatest satisfaction is that Damon has now outlived that bastard." He started to open the door and stopped. "Also, I drink too much sometimes."

"Don't we all," said Clovis. Jeff gave him a thumbs up and closed the door. Interesting, thought Clovis, but something tells me that isn't the whole story. True, Krog was an insensitive, manipulative liar. But he was a taunter, too protective of himself to be downright vicious. He was an outspoken homophobe, but his interaction with Jeff had nothing to do with Gay. There was something Wally had known about Jeff that allowed him to go that step too far. What was it? Jeff was, after all, an actor and Clovis wondered how much of the last scene was a cover up.

Buzz. "Yes, Barbie. Mrs. Krog? Sure, get her for me." Clovis checked his notes. Elizabeth Simpson Krog. Called Betsy. Mother of Wally's three sons. They had been married for twenty-six years, estranged for ten. She was the wife of record.

The voice was high-pitched and fluttery with an almost teenage expectancy. "Mr. Kelley, I've been told that you are conducting the investigation into Wally's death. I think I might have some information of interest to you. Well, most of today I'll be bogged down with the details. There are so many of them. They've taken Wally's body to Riverside. I'm keeping this very private since I don't want those gawking fans that will come to see what actors attend. And the Press. Horrors. But I will be there from seven until ten tonight if you would want to come by. Oh, that would be lovely. Thank you. See you. Ta!"

Clovis wondered if casual clothes would be acceptable and if dinner was included. Obviously, a social occasion. The private wake of a public man.

Knock. A huge man wearing a blue plaid shirt and tired jeans held up by suspenders shuffled in. If it weren't for the Alfred E. Neuman greying head, he could be the model for Frankenstein's monster minus the bolt in neck. His arms hung limply at his side making him seem battery operated.

"I heard (pronounced 'hoid') you looking for killer. It ain't me. That *vonce* what was killed hated me because I'm a Jew. He tried to get me retired. I work good and will not leave until I'm seventy-two when I'm going to Israel. Moe Chernin. Nabet Local 16." And he turned around and shuffled out closing the door behind him.

It seems that I'm very popular and that news travels faster than usual in this strange society. Clovis checked off Moe Chernin, stage hand, and Jeff R. Landon, actor. He clicked on the largest of the four television sets, set it to Channel 6. Business as usual. An unrecognizable Maud Sterling sans wig, with thick glasses, wearing a red jump suit, script in hand was berating Tracy George who had pink rollers in her reddish hair and was wearing a pink sweat shirt and matching jeans and Reebocks. If their fans could see them now! There was something almost obscene about watching the actors in rehearsal. Voyeurism. He checked his Rolex. 11:15. Wally Krog had been dead for twenty-four hours.

# Chapter 4

"Gypsy! Where are you hiding, darling? Mummy doesn't have time to play games today. Gypsy!" A tiny shiny wet black nose shoved itself from under the ecru crocheted lace bedspread of the canopied four poster bed. "There you are, sweetheart," as the rest of the black-and-white miniature Party Poodle emerged, pink bow in top-knot, pink leather rhinestone-studded collar, pompom tail wagging vigorously. Betsy Simpson Krog picked up the four-pound furry body and held it to her breast. Its tiny obsidian eyes shone with adoration. "Come on, sweetness, it's vitamin time."

She carried the animal to the tiny kitchen off the living room. A butcher-block table was covered with neat rows of opaque brown vitamin bottles in an assortment of sizes. She unscrewed the caps of two of the bottles and presented two little pills to Gypsy who chomped them noisily as Betsy watched with pleasure. Then after carefully setting the dog on the patterned linoleum floor, she selected seven bottles, extracted a capsule or pill from each and put them in a waiting saucer. Next she opened the door of the refrigerator that was covered with a crowded display of magnetized vegetable replicas and took out the bottle of acidophilus milk. She swallowed each pill with a sip of the milk, which was therapeutically changing her intestinal flora.

She closed the refrigerator door. The noon ritual was over. Now what was she to do? She wandered aimlessly into the living room and sat in the red velvet wingback chair beside the round mahogany table covered with framed photographs. She stared at

them. Her mother and father in tooled blue leather. Her wedding
picture in silver. A threefold ceramic oval of the boys as babies.
Herself age seven on that dear pony framed in embossed copper.
The glossy publicity picture of Wally taken maybe ten years ago in
the thin steel frame. Automatically, she petted Gypsy who had
arrived on her lap to compete for attention. Betsy's large brown
eyes began to overflow. The first tears she had shed since hearing
the news. Was she crying for Wally, she wondered, or for the
pictorial realities of her life, which did not in any way illustrate
who she really was.

Now what was she to do? Gypsy licked the tears from her
cheeks. She had called Christian and Frederick who were in California. They would be flying in sometime in the afternoon. They
would stay at Wally's. And Johnny, her darling Johnny, had taken
care of all the nasty details.

> KROG - Waldemar, aged 61.
> Beloved husband of Elizabeth
> Simpson Krog, cherished brother
> of Inga, loving father of
> Christian, Frederick and John.
> Services and Internment private.

Nothing was different and yet everything would be. Her "excuse"
was gone. Her reason for thwarting all advances, her alibi for being
faithful was shot down. She had been playing widow for so long,
she only had to cancel the word "grass." Her posture of staying
pure for Wally was now invalidated. And Wally always had been
there to protect her like a benevolent father. With promises to
help. True, he never did but he always promised so very nicely. He
still treated her like the fragile child she was when he had first
seen her.

What would she do now? Grieve? She'd stopped grieving ten
years ago when the separation had become formal—yet oh-so-safe
for both of them. Yes, she would miss Wally. His lies. His gal-

lantry. His vows. His overwrought pleas for help. Yet, for over half her life, he had guided her. Or thought he had. Betsy kissed the top of the dog's head and smiled. "Well, little Gypsy, what Daddy didn't know won't hurt him now." Little Gypsy had been his separation gift so that she could always measure their living apart by Gypsy's age.

"Well, darling, shall we figure out what we're going to wear tonight. Yes, darling, of course it must be black. If we were in Greece I could wear purple. Now let's see." The dog hopped after her as she went to the closet that ran the length of the hall between the living room and the bathroom. She ran through the list of people she had called about the viewing. She had a checkmark by every name.

And for what she was going to tell Mr. Kelley, she had better write it out and memorize it. That way she would forget nothing. She could rehearse it aloud. In the mirror. With props. Now she knew what to do.

Wanda Lou shoved aside the hundreds of eight-by-ten glossies that cluttered the top of her desk as she tried to make room for the paper plates and napkins and classic white containers with luncheons #4 and #7. "I'm so flattered you wanted to have lunch with me on your very first day," Wanda Lou gushed.

"Come on," said Vickie with a raised eyebrow. "Cut the bullshit. It's me, Vickie, a.k.a. Victoria Jessup. Remember me? Why on this very day twenty years ago we tried out for the same part in that Off-Broadway revival of OUR TOWN and neither of us got it."

"You're kidding! Who got the part?"

"The one thing I've always loved most about you, Wanda Lou, is how gullible you are. Do you think I'd remember something like that or what day it was. Honestly. Who else could I lunch with in this place who would answer questions instead of asking them?"

Wanda Lou got up and went around the desk to hug Vickie. "I've missed you."

"And I've missed you. We haven't dished since you came back from California with Jeb. That's almost a month ago. How did it go?" Vickie watched Wanda Lou's lower lip start to quiver. She knew the sign too well. "Sorry. You would have told me if something wonderful had happened."

"He's still out there. Hoping. How can a grown man be such a child?"

"Because he's not a grown man. He's an actor. We had the sense to get out of it. We realized there were other things to do when there were no longer parts for women of a certain age. So what don't I know?"

Wanda Lou patted her rouged cheeks and looked toward the ceiling. "Where to begin? Yancey was not going to renew her contract because she hated the late-lamented so much, but now I think she might. She loves you. And, most important, she's got a new 'fella.' Clovis Kelley who's—he's the one they just put in charge of the investigation. So goodlooking. She seems much happier with him than she did with what's his name—I lose track of Yancey's loves. Oh yes, *big* secret. Tracy's preggers. No one else knows. Now that Wally's gone maybe she'll tell so that you can write it into the story line. She's thrilled. And our "Star's" husband was right cozy with Wally. But you knew that. I almost forgot. Wally caught on to the fact that Max was stuffing the ballot box. You know. He had the same people writing fan letters with different handwritings but they were all mailed from the same place— somewhere in Minnesota. Anyway, Wally figured it out and threatened to tell the Network about it. No, even better, I remember now. He was going to expose him to *TV Guide*. Can you believe it."

Vickie did not look amused. "Yes, I can. But tell me, who was his latest squeeze."

"Well, everyone knows about Jolie. He still had the hots for

Tracy. I think the next victim would have been Heather. She's that new kid they've got to play opposite Tony. She's from Juilliard and very good. Basically from Georgia. And, you know what? I think she's still a virgin."

"Wally must have been slipping," Vickie said shaking her head.

"Well, she was only here for two weeks. Contract. You'll like her. Oh yes, Wally kept hinting that he was seeing someone in 'high places,' which seemed to give him the right to act more disgusting as weeks went on." Wanda Lou caught her breath. "I'm ashamed to admit how glad I am that he's gone."

"You're not alone from everything I've heard. Anything else I should know?"

Wanda Lou closed her eyes as if to run a parade of faces in front of her. "Yes. Watch your back with Nora Easton. I know you brought her in and she was lovey-dovey with you. But she was just the same with Wally only more so. I don't trust her, Vickie."

"Thanks. Well, shall we?" Vickie asked as she extended her hand with the two fortune cookies in it. Wanda Lou took one and snapped it open. "Do you think the person in 'high places' was Allie?" Vickie asked.

"I always thought she had better taste. Listen to this: 'Only you can turn your path into a road.' Honey, I'd like to make it a highway. What's yours?"

Vickie held up the printed slip. "I should keep this one. 'When the teacher is ready, the pupil will appear.' I always thought of it the other way around. Well, I'm ready."

"Are you going to the wake or whatever it is tonight?" asked Wanda Lou. "I'm certainly not dressed for it." She stood up to exhibit her red and blue plaid pants, striped green and white scalloped edged blouse and bright yellow Reeboks with matching socks.

"If I'm asked. I better get back to my cubicle. A lot to do before runthrough. Thanks for the feast and good luck on your road."

Wanda Lou gave Vickie another hug. "I'm real glad you're back. It'll be like old times."

"Hopefully," smiled Vickie. Dear, naive, loving, dumb Wanda Lou. Everytime you nicked her she bled information. Obviously, there was one important fact that she did not have. Thanks God!

When in Rome, thought Clovis, as he dug into Barbie's highly recommended luncheon #3 (Spicy chicken with fried rice, no MSG) while watching today's air show.

Nora had carefully explained to him "I'm so sorry I can't stay and watch it with you but I've got a long standing doctor's appointment and you know how hard they are to get." Parts of today's episode had been taped two weeks previously. Lydia's side of the phone conversation for example, because Lydia had some sort of conflict and the Sheraton Pool Room set wasn't up again until the day before yesterday so they edited the phone call last night. Such a deep mine of information. Truly important stuff. No, there was nothing else she could do for him except go away. He thanked her profusely (too profusely would scare her off) and after yet another nervous smile, she left.

On the screen, the Star strutted about. Right-manicured hand on her swiveling right hip, left-manicured hand combing through her long blond hair. The scene was in the office of lawyer Gray Lansing, played by Jeff R. Landon, which was in lovely downtown Clearview as the backdrop through his bay window showed. He had just advised her not to challenge her estranged husband. She paused, walked slowly toward his eight-foot desk, leaned on it and snarled "Don't worry, I'll make him pay for this." *Extreme Close Up* of her huge mascared blue eyes. Fade to black.

Three ascending harp plucks joined by a lush spread of strings energized by a soft kettledrum beat announced the opening of THE KEY TO LIFE. On the first pluck, a large embossed gold keyhole in a highly polished mahogany door faded in as an anonymous hand holding a large ornate, old fashioned, oversized gold key entered the frame and unlocked the door. Beyond which was another door that opened and then another, as special effects took the doors to infinity with swelling music the name of the show was spelled out in clear gold script. In just 30 seconds. Commercial. A brigade of dancing lemons fills the screen.

The Star bore an uncanny resemblance to Tillie Ryan. The same owl flat face. Clovis wondered if they were related. Act One opened with the "Star" in a shimmering silver negligee that just barely covered her cleavage. Silicone? The contacts helped make her eyes an impossible blue. And, Clairol 97, the natural extra-light beige blonde. He knew she was not Yancey's favorite. Whore playing lady and Yancey was lady playing ex-hooker. Almost a cliché. At least Yancey was believeable. Or was he just a bit prejudiced.

An officious knock and the door opened. The wide shoulders on Marti Livorski's Donna Karan white jacket (wool, silk and polyamide) preceded her. The scent of Giorgio defined her presence. Clovis rose to shake her extended limp right hand with rings on her third and fourth fingers.

"I didn't know what you were planning on your first day or we could have done lunch," she smiled.

"You're Allie Jones' assistant, Marti Livorski," he smiled back.

"My, what a memory." And what a gorgeous hunk. That Yancey really lucked out this time around. "Since KEY is my show, that is, I'm the network liase, I know everything about it. Allie suggested I might be of some help to you. You know, explaining who does what." She spoke carefully emphasizing her "ds" and "ts".

"That's very kind of both of you. Everyone has been very cooperative. Nora Easton has furnished me with a creative assortment of paper that seems to represent how the show works." Clovis gestured to the stacks on the table top.

"Oh, her." (Pronounced 'huh.') "Nora has a tendency to take on more than her plate can hold. And she's not up to speed physically." A concerned look crossed her face. "She's been with the show three years and I don't think she's quite defined her franchise."

Polite try but it did not cover the fact that Nora was not on her best-loved list. "Three years means that she was here when Vickie was."

"Vickie brought her in. She was at one of the other networks in research. Wally didn't have to keep her on but he was very kind."

Clovis looked at her expression to see if she was putting him on. No. Finally, he had found a pro-Krog. "Why was Vickie replaced?"

"I'll put it right on the table. KEY is a very high concept show and Vickie didn't seem to be able to access the idea. No matter how many meetings she took with Allie and me, she didn't seem to be able to glom onto it." She continued to explain, using high-tech phrases that gave her a quick veneer of special intelligence. It all translated to the fact that Allie believed Wally could energize the show by his sheer masculine dynamism.

"And where had Wally been before coming here to produce KEY?"

"He was on the Coast. He directed many episodes on Prime Time. And produced various late night and syndicated shows."

Not very precise. With good reason. Clovis had already examined his loser's resume. Didn't anyone in the business check with previous employers? They seem to take more time checking a maid's references.

"This really is a tragedy. Not only for his family. But for the show. Wally never had a chance to hit his stride." She shook her head. How much did he know, she wondered. "Well, if there's anything else I can help you with. Don't hesitate." A smile lurked at the corners of her mouth.

"I won't."

She seemed about to say something and changed her mind. "I better go see how Vickie's doing." She lingered for another moment. Barbie came in and efficiently removed the remains of his lunch, which seemed to spur Marti out of the room.

What the hell was that all about? Lots of double meanings, a few innuendos, and no substance. Full of sound and fury signifying zilch. And dammit, he didn't even get a chance to read his fortune cookie.

"Well, I sure didn't expect to see you today," Mark mumbled through the hairpins in his mouth, not taking his eyes off the brunette mass of hair he was styling on the wig block.

"Talking to me or that dummy?"

"You, dummy," he answered and turned to Jolie. She was supporting herself against the back of the first barber chair. Hair uncombed. Remnants of yesterday's make-up on her small bird-shaped face. A small, deflated, discarded doll. "I've seen better rejects for Poor Pitiful Pearl."

"That good." And tears began to form in the corners of her eyes.

Mark folded Jolie in his arms. "Why don't you go home?"

"And give these bastards here the satisfaction of thinking his death meant that much to me!" She pulled away from him.

"Well, excuuuse me! Just drown my elegant number 10's in salt water. You see, Arthur," he explained to an imaginary person, "Jolie's taken the Veil. Ooops, sweetie, wrong number. Vale of Tears. Well, she flooded the Hair Room and won the Niobe Contest." Putting his second and third fingers on either side of her mouth, he pushed the corners up, forming a smile. "Lillian Gish to Donald Crisp. Broken Blossoms. But what would you know."

"What did Arthur say?" she asked.

"I'll tell you some other time," he said returning to the wig.

"No. Now. I have to know. I want to know what everyone said."

"Are you sure you don't want to go home. All right, then at least wash your face. For the honor of the Hair Room."

Jolie bent over the shampoo sink and washed her face. Mark came up behind her and poured shampoo over her hair and helped her wash it.

"Well, you know how obliging Arthur is—especially for someone so talented. Anyway, you remember when Wally saw the wallpaper in here and asked me where I got it and I said a friend of mine. And Mr. High-and-Mighty said with his usual emphatic anti-Gay pause, 'your *boy* friend' and I said yes. So he said he needed someone with taste to decorate something. Dissolve. Arthur and Wally meet and he wants Arthur to redo his ex-wife's apartment as a gift for her or somesuch nonsense. Arthur runs around and gets samples and looks at Betsy's apartment and takes Mrs. Off-the-Wall all over town to showrooms and Decorators' walk and God knows where else. And she can't make up her mind but wants to meet again and Arthur is picking up taxi fares and lunches and this goes on for weeks and finally Arthur tells Wally they've almost made a few decisions. And do you know what that, that bastard—sorry Jolie—did? He says thank you to Arthur but they're not going to do anything. He just wanted to lift poor Betsy's spirits because she was a little low. The only reason Arthur ever went along with it was because he didn't want to create a problem for me with my boss. It wasn't even what it cost Arthur in time and out-of-pocket, it was the attitude. Here, slave, amuse one of the Royal Family. No, Jolie, Arthur shed no tears."

"I cry enough for everyone," Jolie said quietly. "Eh bien. C'est fini." She towel dryed her hair.

"Well, Sweetie, you sure washed that man right out of your hair."

"One day you'll go too far," she said flicking the towel at him. "I understand that Yancey's friend is conducting the investigation."

"Yes. And don't tell Arthur I said so, but is he ever gorgeous. That hair. Those teeth. And the rest. I wish I were single again," he sang.

"Someone's happy today," said DeeDee Dakin entering the Hair Room. "Everyone else around here is tiptoeing and whispering and looking over their shoulder. Which one of you will whip my coiffure into shape?"

"I'll do it," said Jolie, lighting a cigarette, and indicating the first barber chair.

"You get all the fun," Mark minced.

DeeDee Dakin, wife of Dewey, was tall, high cheekboned and honey-blond. Once a high fashion model, she had married Dewey on the rebound from a name-whispered, equally-high political figure. She had given Dewey two children. He had given her worship and Southern class and a house in SaltAir on Fire Island and an apartment on Riverside Drive with Gestadt and Paris and Rome for extras. She appeared on KEY whenever the scripts called for rich, ornamental types for social occasions with the uppercrust of Clearview. Dewey saw to it that galas and parties were written in as often as possible. Usually with a line or two for some fashionable slightly older woman. Instead of being an extra with not a word to utter, DeeDee joined the elite "under five" category. Less than five lines to speak but it paid more than an extra. And, there were those special times when she had more than five lines to speak and became a day player. Extra pin money and insurance coverage.

There was less traffic than usual in the Hair Room, out of deference to or fear of the bereaved Jolie. There was only Max Arden in Mark's chair as Jolie worked listlessly on DeeDee. Nora Easton paused on the threshold, left hand gracefully holding the collar of her dark green and red plaid shirt, right hand clutching her green leather spring binder with the show's name elegantly tooled in gold (last year's Christmas gift from the Network). She watched Jolie. A cigarette was anchored in her mouth, an occasional tear flowed out of her smoke-squinted eyes as she apathetically brushed DeeDee's long, honey-blond hair.

Brows furrowed in sympathy, Nora asked, "Jolie, why don't you go home?"

"Why the hell should I?" Jolie challenged, brushing the hair with renewed vigor.

"I just thought that you would be more—"

"I would be more what? More what? If I am miserable, what difference does it make where I am miserable? At least here I am miserable and get paid. So no thank you very much," she added, her accent thickening.

"I was just trying to be helpful," Nora persisted.

"Then go the fuck away."

"Right on," Mark mumbled as he moussed Max Arden's grand white pompadour.

"Ouch!" said DeeDee.

"Sorry," said Jolie to her.

Saint Nora The-Put-Upon straightened her shoulders and looked in the mirror at DeeDee, hoping for some affirmation of her thoughtfulness. None was forthcoming. Well! She had better things to do than play wet-nurse to Wally's used toy. And as for that no-talent demanding wife of that no-talent henpecked writer, they would be out on their snob asses when she was through.

In her dressing room, Tracy George tugged at the dark blue padded collapsible chair that was supposed to pull open and flatten into a cot arrangement. Like everything else supplied by those cheap bastards at the United Broadcasting System, it didn't work. Damn. Tears of frustration welled in her eyes. She was tired and wanted to lie down. Was that too much to ask, Oh God? She'd be damned if she would ask anyone for help and admit she wasn't strong enough to open the monster. "What's the matter? Didn't you sleep last night? Got the flu? Got the bug? Got your period? Get laid last night?" A string of predictably stupid questions from stupid people who didn't give a damn anyway. One of her favorite ploys was to answer their it's-none-of-your-business questions with total non sequitors. It proved that no one listened. Which proved they did not care. And the true answer to why she was feeling queasy now and wanted to rest would start an avalanche of questions and advice. Two months pregnant, but she didn't want anyone in the Studio to know yet.

Yes, she had told Wanda Lou who, for all her dittsiness, was well grounded in the realities of actors' problems and contracts. And, she did have a heart. Strange in this shark tank called KEY. Wanda Lou had discovered Tracy seven years ago when she'd been standing by in CRIMES OF THE HEART. Tracy had never done television before and Wanda Lou, forever empathetic, had coached her in the differences in acting on stage (large) to being in front of a camera (small). She had counseled her on what to wear and how to conduct herself during the interviews. And, Tracy had gotten the role: Samantha (Sam) Dowling, the illegitimate daughter of Lydia Sheraton (played by Maud Sterling) who had given her up at birth. Samantha was brought on the show as perky, classy, feisty, fun-living, rebellious, aggressive, and feminine—a role model for the eighties ladies. She had started as a stranger to Clearview, a physical therapist hired by Dr. Milo Sheraton, who fell in love with her before it was revealed that he was her brother. She then went through a series of professions in her six years on KEY that ran the gamut from cub reporter to club hostess until her latest stint as a cop. Sam's romantic entanglements only rivaled those of the "Star," with whom she had several love triangles. Both vying for the same romantic object.

In Tracy's real life she had met and married the sweet, now balding Jack Himmelfarb, whose name appeared on the mastheads of more failed magazines than there were failed shops on Columbus Avenue. Father-to-be of Baby currently without sex or name. Wanda Lou had agreed that, with Wally in charge, it would not be smart to mention the pregnancy. She advised Tracy to wait until she started to show and then approach Tillie, who was a sentimental pushover. Tillie was also the creative one and would know how to handle this complication and write it into the story line in such a way that it would become an "event." Perhaps keep the identity of Sam's baby's father a great secret so the fans could try to guess who it was. God knows Dewey didn't have the imagination. He would panic and suggest an abortion so that his precious outline would not have to be tampered with. As for Wally, he would most likely rev up the action scenes in hopes that she might have a real miscarriage.

Tracy knew that it was thanks to Wally that she did not have a desk job as a cop. Oh no. Wally loved remotes, he loved getting out of the Studio to avoid its routine. Also, he revelled in the free hotel rooms, drink, food, cars as well as the opportunity to seduce any female stranded with him and the rowdy crew of his followers. Running, jumping, crouching, climbing—Tracy could not take any more physically. A shoot-out across a dune in Amagansett, a drug bust up and down the stairs of a Harlem tenement, a foot race in Soho, across tar beach roof tops in the West 80's. Enough. She wanted this baby and at thirty-three she was heading for her clock to run down. What if she and Jack wanted another? They were both only children who wanted more than one child. Tracy, like Sam, was used to getting what she wanted. She had not been about to let Wally get her written off the show because she couldn't handle the physical aspects of the role as he had it defined in his head. No way. Without her income, they could not afford to have the baby. She would never have given him that option. Never.

A quick knock at her dressing room door. That would be Maud. She wearily raised herself and opened the door.

"Tracy, you've been resting. I'm so sorry. Are you all right?"

"I'm fine, Maud."

"Would you mind if I used your phone?" Maud indicated the pale blue Trimline on the makeup shelf.

"Help yourself," said Tracy. How she longed to have the courage to tell her that she was tired of being interrupted. That she wished she'd get her own fucking phone instead of tieing up the lines in the make-up room and the hair room and her dressing room. How cheap can you get?

"Thank you, dear. There are too many eager ears out there. Especially today. I won't be a moment." She picked up the phone receiver and waited.

"I have to go to make-up anyway," said Tracy politely as she left her dressing room.

Maud quickly jabbed seven numbers and nervously waited for the ringing to stop. "Thank heaven you're there. It's been very strange today. I'd love to make it tonight," she purred, "but I don't think it wise. I don't know who I'll be saddled with after the funeral parlor. Mr. Kelley is in charge. Anyway. Love you. Take care." She hung up the phone and looked at herself in the dressing-room mirror. She placed her hands against her cheeks and pressed up. Not so bad for an old girl. She winked at herself, waved at her reflection and left the dressing room.

# Chapter 5

"Now, Mr. Kelley—I mean Clovis?" Barbie Dixon asked eagerly as she bounced into the office.

Clovis scratched along the top of his right cheek where his sideburn used to be. Yancey's hand was not there to slap his and say, "Nasty habit!" And then he'd take her hand and kiss it and then—"Sorry, Barbie, what did you say?"

"I didn't yet. I wanted to know if now was a good time to tell you all the story lines and stuff about KEY like you asked before." She was so excited by the prospect that she was almost on point in her black Nikes.

"Tell you what," said Clovis rising and cat-stretching his back, "I'd like a breath of air to clear my head. Let me take a quick hike around the block and I will be able to concentrate on your every word." He picked up his black tweed jacket that was hung behind the chair and slung it over his shoulder.

"Super." Barbie called after him. "I'll get someone to cover the phones. Now don't you run away."

Clovis smiled at her enthusiasm. My God! Was anyone that young anymore? Or was she slightly retarded. He walked swiftly past Barbie's station, a small enclosed area that protected her from messengers and separated her from a cluster of worn grey sofas that flanked Wanda Lou's office. They were usually crammed with actors but there was no activity today. The atmosphere of the entire Studio was hushed, expectant.

He ran down the front stairs, through the front glass door and crossed the street to get a better perspective of the building that housed THE KEY TO LIFE. It was a short, squat, two-story sprawl made of once yellow pre-fab bricks now weathered to tan. Taking up most of the block between Columbus and Amsterdam Avenues, it was topped by an uneven black tar roof. Three huge television dishes were planted at odd angles, looking like three giant women obscenely raising their pleated white skirts to the sky. Hoping to catch the first falling alien?

As Clovis had learned, the Studio Three building was quite self-contained. Practically everyone and everything that went into the production of Channel 8's most successful daytime drama was right there. The front fan-infested glass entrance lead to that small reception area where the uniformed guard's monotony was relieved by watching the huge television set opposite forever tuned to Channel 8. The guard registered visitors, called actors to the "lobby," disseminated messengers and gave dressing room keys to the actors. Familiar faces from United Broadcasting's roster of executives or engineers sometimes were requested to show IDs. Usually not. The door to the right of the guard lead to a staircase to the second floor cum landing and then on to the roof. A door to the left opened onto a long hall with lots of doors on either side.

As Clovis walked around the block slowly, he mentally walked the hall. On the right was Male Wardrobe, then Female Wardrobe, a few dressing rooms, an open staircase to the second floor. Oh, yes, at the bottom of the staircase was a mail-box arrangement for scripts and messages with slots for each contract member of the cast. Next came the Make-Up Room, then the Hair Room, a few more dressing rooms and the His-and-Hers toilets, complete with three stalls, two sinks, and one shower. Opposite was the back staircase cum landing that led to the second floor.

Good physical exercise. Good mental exercise. Coming back down the hall were a few dressing rooms, then the Audio and Music Room, then a short corridor with double doors that lead to the Studio. Then there was the door to the Control Room, then the Video Room and another door to the Studio. And that was where all the action took place. Clovis stopped on the street opposite the back of the building. Huge warehouse doors opened into the Scene Dock, which, in turn, had elephant doors that opened onto the Studio. During the night, it was here that the scenery and props were loaded and unloaded as each day's required sets were put up and furnished. Truly a mammoth operation. To the left was a human-size door that actors sometimes used to escape from their fans. That door was always open during the day. Anyone known to the crew could arrive through it without any problem. Or leave?

Wally's death could have been on impulse. But it was no accident. No stage hand with a grudge, nor a neurotic actor would take the kind of chance necessary to attack in an arena as public as a working studio. It had to be someone driven to such a pitch of intense hatred that s/he had been blind to everything but the need to stop Wally's clock. A hatred fed by sufficient adrenalin to shove a 10-inch knitting needle—without a finely honed point—straight through Wally's thick neck. The medical examiner's report had verified that the #3, on a lucky thrust, was indeed the murder weapon. Technically, it was made of a steel-like substance called Silvalume manufactured under the "Susan Bates" logo. #11110. 3 1/4mm. Of an unattractive lavender hue. The needle's owner was Maggie List, the gray-haired character actress who played Lily Edgerton. She was not on today's show. It was common knowledge that Maggie and her knitting were inseparable. It was also used as a character trait on the show. Mme. De Farge?

As Clovis headed back, he reviewed the second floor. Beyond Wanda Lou was the Production Office that leads to Gina Serpente's tiny space and the Xerox room. That was on the left. Wally's office faced it on the right. Then the inevitable corridor with the Actors' Lounge to the left with the Lighting Grid beyond that. The Editing Room came next opposite the interior staircase.

Then the Rehearsal Hall on the left, Engineers' Lounge on the right. At the end, beyond a few more dressing rooms, was a warren of small offices. They belonged to the Unit Manager, the Studio Manager, the Tech Manager, and the Directors. In the planners' infinite wisdom, none of these small offices had windows. The window side was occupied by Wardrobe storage. A His and a Hers sans showers. The back staircase. And, with the exception of the dressing rooms, there was not an office too small for a television set.

Something was missing. But, of course. He'd forgotten Nora Easton's office, which was next to Wally's. She was easy to forget. Since her early morning assault, she had not returned to offer her services. Busy, busy, busy. And that's what he'd better get. Start winnowing down the suspect list from several hundred to a comfortable ten or twenty. Thank heaven he was sufficiently knowledgeable of a studio's workings not to be overwhelmed by all the titles and their corresponding functions. No wonder poor little Napoleon Kaufman had bowed out so quickly. He had better begin to define and then refine some motives. After all, as Yancey's "fella," he had to uphold his reputation and not let her down.

And then he remembered his last conversation with Wally. He had blocked it almost immediately. Completely. He had not wanted Yancey to know about it. He'd been so damned mad that he had suddenly craved a cigarette for the first time in months. It took enormous self control not to bum one and inhale deeply again and again. That might have calmed him enough to lose the itch to deck Wally. And then kick him. Hard. In the balls. Goddamn that man! Well, someone already had. Wally had an uncanny knack of knowing the exact button to push to get anyone's sensibilities perverted into a howling rage.

Clovis had degaussed—erased the tape—like it never happened. Yet now, remembering, he could still feel the gut kick he had experienced. Come on! There he was a reasonable, soon-to-be fifty-six year-old adult, maybe about to fall in love for the second

—okay third—time in his life. He was quite successful, more than financially well off. And yes, he knew he looked like an actor —what ever that meant—to the hundred or so people who accused him of looking like one. Writing a book he was enjoying. And that two-bit tin-horn Scandavanian fake had reduced him to a childlike fury.

Two weeks ago, he was angrier than he had ever been in his life. It was when an ex-ex beau of Yancey's, an actor turned head soap-opera writer, was having one of his Sunday nights. Yancey explained to Clovis how they had met when she first came to New York, a frightened kid from Texas. David (never Dave) Bigelow had been a waiter at Joe Allen's while looking for an acting job. They had gone on auditions together, helping each other, and, as two lonely kids, had a few romantic interludes to comfort each other. They had remained friends since then and David had been dying to meet Clovis to make sure Yancey was being done right by.

"Makes me sound like a stud," he protested.

"What's wrong with that? Lighten up." David had a few special friends over the first Sunday of every month. A bit of booze, a bite of hors d'oeuvre. Hang loose. Stay long or short. "David may seem gay but he's not. Maybe a little Bi under the right auspices. He's a nice, decent guy who's worked hard for his version of success. And now that he can afford to, he loves indulging himself. He's a believer in 'right things.' Orange County, California. You know the type. I promise we don't have to stay for more than a drink. Mr. Kelley, we cannot be hermits."

"Why not?" he had asked.

"You're just saying that to get me angry because you like to see me angry because for some perverted reason it turns you on. Right?"

"Right. So pay up and I'll go." She did.

David lived in an Americana antiques-decorated basement duplex in Chelsea. A lightfooted waiter passed the smoked salmon on pumpernickel dotted by a caper, the bacon-wrapped sausages and the curried chicken wings. His seeming twin circulated champagne in fluted glasses. A pine sideboard was jammed with cheeses, salamis and shrimp. Nice.

A tall, slender, bearded man, David greeted them wearing a green silk caftan which, as he explained, he had specially woven for him in Tunisia. "So you're the California hater. Congratulations. Someone who hates California and loves Yancey can't be all bad. Which arm did she have to twist to get you here?"

"Both," smiled Clovis, very aware that a beaming Yancey looked from former to current lover.

"I'm very glad to meet you because I've been admirer of yours for quite some time. Your book. I can't tell you how helpful it has been to me."

How could you not like a guy who has not only read your book but liked it. "What a nice way to meet you. Thanks."

"You may see a few familiar faces. I like to mix and match. Don't you drink?" he asked as Clovis indicated no to the champagne tray.

"One of my favorite sports. But not champagne."

"Hey, it's an open bar. What can I get you?"

"Absolut on a lot of rocks."

David left him to get the drink. Yancey, Clovis saw, drink in hand, was talking with Maud Sterling, who he had met at the Studio. Handsome woman, vibrant, sparkling. She was wearing her "Lydia" wig, which made her seem younger than her admitted sixty-two years. She pirouetted as the waiter went by with a tray of drinks, depositing an empty and picking up a full without his having to stop. Graceful. There were a few familiar faces from the show that he had watched whenever Yancey was on. A many-faceted woman. The "Star" and her husband arrived. David, the compleat host, maneuvered her and her heel-clicking husband over to Clovis and introduced them. "I can't believe you haven't met," he smiled and handed Clovis his drink.

Tossing her long blond mane, the "Star" smiled. "I hear you and Yancey met in California. I adore it. It's one of our dreams to live there, isn't it, darling?" she asked the husband who seemed to be counting the house and looking for someone more influential than Clovis with whom to exchange pleasantries. The "Star" tossed her head again and Clovis realized who she was emulating. Not consciously, he hoped. He couldn't wait to tell Yancey.

Clovis was mercifully saved from further conversation by a woman with birds' nest hair and Annie Hall layers of clothing who pounced on the "Star," kissing both of her painted cheeks. She then turned and introduced herself to Clovis. Allie Jones. She'd heard so many wonderful things about him. She had an idea she was going to meet him today. What a pleasure. She spoke in little half-sentence bird chirps. She'd come with Wally Krog who materialized as she spoke his name.

"Clovis. Clovis Kelley. I see you two know each other," he said playing host.

"We've just met," said Allie. "Oh, there's Maud. I must say hello." And off she flew.

"Well, Mr. Clovis Kelley," he repeated the name as if trying to say it without an accent. "It is always good to see you. There is something I would like to ask you." Taking Clovis by the elbow, he steered him out to the garden which was festooned with large dripping candles. "Lovely setting, isn't this, that Dave has here?"

"Very well done," agreed Clovis, knowing from his own garden how difficult it was to keep one manicured and alive. And expensive!

"I realize that you are no longer connected with the Police Department. But certainly a man like you keeps his connections alive. It would be no more than a telephone call from a man like you to the right person. And then we—you and I, that is—would be able to do the most spectacular remote that a television serial has ever done." He put his arm around Clovis' shoulder in an old buddy gesture. "I know that you would like to make THE KEY

TO LIFE better and better. Why? Because Yancey is on the show and whatever is good for the show is good for Yancey. Now isn't that right?" He stepped back and started to gesture as he described the various shots of a three-car chase on both levels of the 59th Street Bridge. It would end with one car hurtling into the East River followed by the brave rescue of the actor—he was not certain, as yet, which story line it would best serve—trapped in the car.

He was talking so fast that his accent thickened as his tongue seemed to catch making the words garbled. "I am such a brilliant planner that I believe we could do the entire episode in the morning of one day. Certainly as a man of vision you can see what I'm after. And, of course, I can make the network give you a credit." Wally nodded his head in Allie's direction. "People like you who have all the money in the world do not need monetary kudos. But a big credit and all the publicity. It would all accrue. Surely, you cannot say no to me about this." As Clovis said nothing, he continued. He moved closer to Clovis. "You know, if you were to help me, I could be very helpful to Yancey. I would make them examine her contract. Maybe a few more bucks. Maybe even extend it for another year."

The presumption of the bastard. All under the guise of flattery. Making him a pimp and Yancey a pawn without a smidgeon of respect. He could not be dismissed merely as insane because the son-of-a-bitch knew what he was doing. His ego shone through his pale blue eyes behind the rimless bifocals. What made it so galling was that behind the words was a challenge, a mockery. He wanted to see how much he could manipulate and get away with. His next ploy would be sarcasm, caricature. Expressionless, Clovis stared at him. Just stared. His look was so cold, Wally was forced to drop his eyes.

"Well," he said, giving Clovis a patronizing pat on the arm, "think it over." And he walked away.

David put a fresh drink in Clovis' hand. "I have a feeling you could use this."

"Thanks. You don't miss much. I'd love to know what broken mechanism makes that bastard tick." He took a long swallow of the vodka.

"Sorry. I didn't invite him but I'm too much of a gent to turn him away at the door. Allie still lives in a world that thinks she cannot go anywhere unescorted. But the stories I could tell you about Wally . . ."

"I wondered where you guys were," said Yancey. "What's up?" She looked at Clovis with such loving tenderness, he couldn't resist a full kiss. "Ain't he something?" she asked David.

"Don't answer that, please," Clovis laughed. "And now I've got the revelation of the age for both of you. Your so-called "Star"— why didn't you tell me she's modelled herself after Miss Piggy?"

"I wish I'd said that," laughed David.

"In the words of the great: 'You will, Oscar, you will'," smiled Clovis. And with Yancey's repressed hoot and loving hug, Clovis had erased Wally's entire proposition.

Now, two weeks later, Clovis remembered their exchange. Wally could really goad anyone. He'd once read that "it was easier to milk a bat than to predict what may attract a poet. Some inexplicable blend of temperament, style, compulsion and accident." That was also true of murderers. He made a mental note to add David Bigelow to the list of people with whom he should discuss the reasons for the murder of Waldemar Krog, Producer.

Engineers' hangout. Euphemistically "Lounge." It was an oblong space furnished with the worn couches and tables discarded from the rehearsal hall. Against one wall was a battered metal clothes-rack with a few jaunty bent-wire hangers next to an ancient green-streaked refrigerator with a broken door handle. A huge dented coffee urn rested on what in a previous life had been a bridge table. It was adorned with styrofoam cups, packets of sugar products, stirrers and a carton of milk never put in the fridge for fear it would absorb the varying odors of the stashed brown-bag lunches. The simple wall decor was a large cork bulletin board pin stabbed with schedules, a few Polaroids of bowling outings, Union bulletins and NO SMOKING signs. And, the inevitable television set.

"Hey, man, watch. It's the next shot. Now ain't that one fan-fucking-tastic rack focus!" Lester Williams, Camera 3, demanded of Francis (Frank) Quinn, Camera 2 as the on screen closeup of Jingo blurred and Bart's head went from blur to clear.

"Yeah," it's a good shot," Frank agreed, "but it only worked because Chuck knew how to set it up to go from Jingo to Bart so that it made a story point. We could rack focus on every fucking shot from who knows what to what but if it ain't making a point, it don't mean nothing."

"Look, it's fine for you guys to discuss last week's shots, but me, I wanna know what's gonna happen now that Wally's been offed?" Roseann deNapoli, Camera One, asked them.

"Whaddaya mean?" asked Frank as he slowly got up from the couch where the three of them were slouched, their stretched jean-covered legs crossankled, Addidas resting on the coffee table. He rose to his full, broad-shouldered six-foot-five.

"You know how Wally always said about how he put this hand-picked crew together. And how he always had to fight to defend us against them muckymucks at UBS Headquarters who was always trying to split us up," Roseann asked. "Now do we get shook up and get separated and sent off to different shows all over?"

"More of Wally's bullshit. Fucking windbag," said Frank. He pushed the handle on the coffee urn and poured some into a cup.

Roseann turned her sallow face to Lester with a puzzled look. Lester, a handsome, slight, black man shrugged his shoulders.

"Look, you gotta remember I ain't been here as long as you guys. I never met Vickie before today. All you guys are hugging her and saying welcome home. I ain't never seen her before," Roseann explained.

"So answer the lady," Lester said.

"This coffee is piss. Remember how he promised that we was going to have a real nice Lounge." Frank took another swallow. "I guess today ain't the day to complain about coffee." He looked at the two of them studying him. "Wally was always making promises. It was easier than saying no."

"So," Lester prompted.

"Comeon, Les, you know as well as I do that Wally had zip to do with putting this crew together. Vickie started it and Arnie followed through. Especially when Wally came on board, Arnie, as technical director, wanted the best fucking crew possible to make his life easier. He worked on the Tech Manager and pulled in a few favors higher up. That's why we're all here—camera, boom, cable pullers—name it. The only thing Wally ever did was promise. And stand in my way."

Roseann sat up sharply. Even without her headset, she looked like a pixie. Thin-shouldered, flat-chested, she didn't seem to have the physical strength necessary to push and pull the heavy pedestal camera or the long, unwieldy cables. She remembered being interviewed by Wally who insisted on feeling her arm muscles. Everytime he'd come on the floor, he would cop a feel of her muscles. As Frank turned away from them, she realized that there was something heavy going on. "Frank, I promise on my mother's grave," she said seriously, making a two fingered sign of the cross across the front of her KEY TO LIFE T shirt, "I promise not to tell no one."

Lester turned to her. "Shit, woman, you're dumb enough to be a nigger."

"I don't like that kind of talk," she said sternly. "If he don't wanna tell me that's one thing, but you don't use no words like that. You got mad enough at Wally when he said that."

"That was him. I'm me," said Lester. "As a black man, I can say anything . . ."

"Shaddup," Frank broke in. "Look, Roseann, I like to do Sports. It breaks up the monotony of the soap, I make a few extra bucks, and doing the games is a challenge. And Sports is always asking for me. But Wally wouldn't ever let me out. He'd fight it."

"But why?" asked Roseann.

"Because," Lester explained, "there's no one else on the whole fucking crew who not only is strong enough but knows how to handle a Steadycam. Wally couldn't have done one of those remotes without Frank. Just think of the times you've seen Frank perched on a ladder with a camera on his shoulder. He can use a handheld camera, which saves using a crane." He then turned to Frank, "Now big boy, you could've gotten out if you really wanted."

"I guess so," Frank admitted, "but then he kept promising."

"What?" Roseann urged.

"Most guys like me—like you, Les, they want to be a Technical Director or a Tech Manager. Or, maybe go into management as a network executive. But me, I always had a different—I guess you could call it a dream. I always wanted to be a director. I even majored in drama at Carnegie Tech. When I got out of college, I worked for a local station in Pittsburgh. One day the cameraman gets sick and they let me take over. Local news. Just set it and zoom when the control room says 'close-up.' So anyway, I'm on camera and there was this football game. Why am I going on? Forget it. I needed the dough and never had the time to learn how to become a director. So Wally finds this out and said I should go to Acting class so I can talk actor talk and he'll give me a break as soon as possible. So I went to Acting class and came back and Wally says next week, next month, next, next. . . . first he blamed—what's the point. It never happened. And now I know it never would."

Roseann went over to Frank who had turned away from them,

head down. She tapped his shoulder. "Anyone home?" He turned around slowly. "Frank, you can't give up. Did you ever tell anyone but Wally?"

"Nah."

"So tell someone. Really. Tell Vickie. The Directors. Chuck's a good guy maybe he'll help. Maybe they'll let you watch rehearsals or sit in the Control Room."

"Thanks, Roseann, you may be right."

"The gentle giant," laughed Lester.

"That's Don Williams," said Roseann.

That woman has but no humor, thought Lester. No wonder Wally never bothered her. She was too dumb to understand. And certainly not goodlooking enough. "Frank," he asked, "did you see anything at all when Arnie asked you to reposition your camera?"

"Nada," said Frank. "I've been thinking all morning that someone on the floor had to see something. He didn't drop from the flies."

"Maybe the boom guys saw something. They're up high on those platforms" suggested Roseann.

"Cameras and booms, cameras and booms," Arnie's voice blasted over the P.A. system.

"Okay, fellas, time to hit the floor," said Lester and they headed toward the back staircase to get to the Studio.

The radio was tuned to her favorite station, Country and Western. She still loved the music, even after growing up in Lubbock, Texas. She studied to it from grammar school to S.M.U. And now she studied scripts with it as background. The first strain told her the song and she turned up the volume to harmonize along with the Gatlins. "All The Gold In California" certainly was one hell of a dumb "our song." In California *she* had struck gold with Clovis.

Yancey had always been very obliging about making guest appearances on other Channel 8 shows. It was the old publicity gimmick of one show using the other to supposedly boost ratings on both. Most actors did the guest shots grudgingly because it put their intelligence and ability to walk and talk at the same time to a strenuous test. For Yancey it was a challenge. She enjoyed meeting her fans, who always remarked on "how much prettier she was in real life," "how very down to earth," how different she was from her character, Sally Deering Brown Cartright, so she "must be a real actress." What the hell, it was a free First Class trip that broke up the KEY routine. And, all the hands-on ego feeding literally meant a longer life for Sally. It also paid off in handsome chuckles all the way to the bank.

Yancey was a particular favorite on COMPARISONS because she could sing almost any audience request a cappella. The show's host (an aging queen passing as a lecher complete with rounded toupee) always made the same observations about Yancey's anatomy, which allowed him to drop Dolly Parton's name as if they were old friends. Then Yancey blushed, the audience whistled, and the host put his arm around her waist.

She had first seen Clovis across the crowded luggage carousel of American Airlines flight #29 that had arrived a little ahead of its scheduled 10:26 P.M. He stood out in the crowd because he kept far back from the bag grabbers. He lit a cigarette with a gold Zippo, eyes trained on the top of the black band where the luggage was being regurgitated into its downward plunge. He looked vaguely familiar. An actor on a TV series? He moved easily, loosely, in slow motion. Tired because she had not slept on the plane and it was pushing two o'clock her time, she closed her eyes. And he was gone.

They met the next afternoon. It was the obligatory yearly lunch with her California agent who always arranged nice sit-down lunches for twelve. He now resided in a simple three-million-dollar shack in Malibu. "Not exactly in the Colony. It's a little closer to Trancas. Less worry about mud slides. 38004 Pacific Coast Highway. You sure I can't pick you up. Taxi? Fine. I'll get you a ride back." Whatever overdecorated, museum-perfect house he lived in, she took pleasure in knowing that she had paid for some part of it.

Clovis Kelley was the beauty's name. He offered the ride back immediately after the coffee, which was as much as she could take. She had two requests. That he not smoke. And that he turn the radio on his '78 Seville to KZLA, 93.3. FM. "All the gold in California . . .".

SHE: Didn't I see you last night at LAX?

HE: Yes. Why were you got up in dark glasses, hair hidden in a brown and beige Skippy cap, and an oversize coat that would have tented Divine?

SHE: I love my fans but when I'm ready for them. Privacy!

HE: Fans?

SHE: I'm an actress. I do a soap called THE KEY TO LIFE. What are you in?

HE: Trouble, obviously. I don't watch—

SHE: Daytime TV or soaps. What are—

HE: I'm no actor. I'm a writer who used to be a cop. And a sometime consultant on TV shows. I'm basically from New York. I shoot back there whenever I can. Don't much like it here. Thinking of heading back for good soon.

SHE: Good. I'm only out here for three more days. Where do you live out here?

HE: I never thought you'd ask. One visit is worth ten thousand words.

He took his eyes off the road long enough to meet her gaze. They grinned at each other. The rest was history. Sometimes she replayed it. Was Clovis finally the answer to her thirty-six-year-old longings.

Ring! Oh, not again. I'll tell that creep. "Listen you," she said into the phone.

"Yancey, it's me. Take it easy," said Clovis.

"Sorry, I thought it was that creep again. Are you through already? What time is it? I can be ready in two shakes."

"Whoa. Relax. It's about four-oh-seven and twenty seconds to be exact. I wondered if you'd gotten anymore of those hangups."

"No, thank God. My only real hang-up is you. Sounds like a song title doesn't it?" she laughed.

"For your kind of music. Also, I think it would be better if I get to the funeral parlor early and spend a little time with Miss Betsy. The invitation read from seven to ten so I think I'll get there like a quarter of seven," he said.

"And you'd prefer getting there alone and having me meet you there about seven-thirtyish," she volunteered.

"Smart. So you will join me there he said ghoulishly."

"Gladly, she said girlishly."

"I'm wearing a black tweed jacket and boring grey flannels."

"I think I might be able to recognize you. I'll be wearing a very simple black sheath. And a red carnation. But I won't tell you where," she teased.

"Good thing I'm a working detective."

"Don't overdo," she admonished. "Kisses. Love you."

And once again he found himself about to act like what he would have considered an asshole just a few months back.

"Clovis, now that you're off the phone, can I come in?" Barbie asked sweetly, perched at the threshold.

"Okay, Barbie, this is your moment, girl."

*I guess I have to go to see old Wally for one last time this evening, thought the murderer. I wonder if they're going to put him away smirking, smiling or sneering. It was impossible to imagine an expressionless Wally.*

# Chapter 6

Conspiratorially, Barbie closed the door and sat down opposite Clovis, nodding with appreciation as she saw he had a pen poised at the top of a long yellow legal pad. Unfortunately stylish in black Capezio leotards with a fitted yellow tunic ending a few inches above her plump knees, Barbie looked like a gross bumble bee. Her broad, round, beaming face reminded Clovis of those yellow sun-shaped stickers with upward grins.

"So you're the KEY expert," Clovis said after she hadn't said anything for a few moments.

"Wally used to call me the 'walking encyclopedia of facts and figures'."

"So let's have a few," Clovis prodded.

"I've got to admit I've only been watching the show for eleven years. When I was eight I was taken sick and my Mom made me stay in bed a whole week and that's when I got onto it. But I read up on everything that happened before then so I can tell you anything you want to know."

"Realistically, I don't think it would be possible to get fifteen years of stories in the time I have. So, give me the salient, the main important points," he added to clarify it for her. "You be the judge."

Barbie puffed up a bit and began. "KEY takes place in Clearview, but it really takes after a town just outside of Doylestown, Pennsylvania where Tillie comes from. She chose that because it's like any small town in the U.S.A. They call it Clearview because they don't like to say where it really is so they can make their own rules about hanging people or anything."

"Hanging people?" Clovis asked.

"You know, arresting or anything. See, if it really takes place somewhere and everybody knows where the place is, then they have to follow the rules of the place. Rules for getting married, laws for arresting criminals, for courtroom scenes. This way they can invent whatever rule or law they want and can change it every year if it needs to be changed. This way Tillie and the writers make up all the laws so they get to work for the stories."

"That certainly would make it easier. Unfortunately, those of us in the real world haven't got it that good," Clovis smiled. "Utopia."

"Huh?"

"An ideal state with perfect laws, a book by Sir Thomas More. Forget it. Just an expression. Go on."

"One of the richest people in Clearview is Lydia Sheraton—she owns all of Clearview and lives in a great mansion that looks like a castle on the top of the hill. We've got a picture of it that we show from time to time which was really taken in Upstate New York, but anyway she owns a Rolls and has lots of servants for everything. She's always fighting with the other rich guy in Clearview, Dwight Edgerton, who owns the Clearview National Bank. They've known each other since they were kids and then she went away and came back and they didn't get married like her parents wanted so they've been enemies ever since and that's very exciting because they're always playing mean tricks on each other." She paused for approval.

"Quite a set up," Clovis encouraged.

"Awesome," she agreed. "That's why KEY is so good. It's about breaking laws and secrets and falling in love and strangers that some people know and some don't and triangles. And it changes every couple of months and sometimes they're the same stories but they happen to different people which makes them different.

And when they run out of steam they bring on a new character or one that was once related that nobody knew about or lost or bring back somebody everybody thought was dead but wasn't and when they come back they're all surprised because the couples are different and when they kill somebody but like them they bring them back as a twin." It was non-stop and Barbie paused to catch her breath.

"And what's going on now?" Clovis asked.

Barbie took a deep breath, got her second wind and started again. "Well, it's about Lily who loves Dwight who is in love with Sally, who is in love with Gray, the lawyer, who is in love with Sam, now a cop, who is in love with Bart, who is in love with Jingo who is in love with Jingo but attracted to Milo. And Sally is divorcing Wayne Cartwright who was Lily's son by another marriage but he disappeared in the deep jungle last year and Bart's mother who was Gray's first wife ran off and only Lily who was once a nurse has the answer to who his father is. She's married to Dwight. Okay?"

"Awesome!" said Clovis. Buried in some part of her mysterious, tiny brain was a perfect recorder tuned to KEY.

"That's kind of it, unless you want to know more of the details but I figure you haven't got enough time for all of them," she said wistfully.

"You're quite right. But I am truly grateful to you for this much. Tell me, Barbie, who do you consider to be the stars or star of the show?"

"There are no stars. All the contract players are equal. That's why they're listed alphabetically on the crawl."

How to put it, he wondered. "Yet," he began, "it's been brought to my attention that a certain female actress—Zoe Zangwill to be exact—is sometimes referred to as 'The Star'."

"Nah. That started with Wally who was always sucking up to her and telling her that. She's been on the show—along with Maud and Max—since Day One. That's all. She keeps threatening to leave but she never will. Her husband won't let her," Barbie added. So this little dumpling knew more than the story lines, Clovis realized. "As a matter of fact what the Network, the people at United Broadcasting, measure is the Fan Mail."

"Fan Mail?"

"You know, the letters that each of the actors get. I get to keep a list of all the letters that come in. And, once a month, I write beside their names how many letters they get. But that's not always the way to tell. Like Max has a club and they write him every month. It's the same people all the time so it really shouldn't count. I'll show it to you," Barbie offered.

"Later," said Clovis wondering why Nora had not supplied him with that list along with the hundreds of others. "And I do promise that if I have any questions, I'll ask you."

"Oh, I've got the answers. I even settle bets between the writers. I settled a big one between Tillie and Dakin. He was wrong! But then he usually is."

Clovis resisted an impulse to give this sincere child a great hug for fear it would be misunderstood. When and if she lost some of that baby fat, she might just be passable. Physically. He didn't hold out much hope for her mental growth.

They had taken a vote and she had lost. Even her darling Johnny had not sided with her. When Wally was alive, it was usually three to two. Would she be all by herself now? She still couldn't see what was so wrong about taking Gypsy to the funeral parlor. No one but the boys would know. And Wally. Gypsy went everywhere with her, hunkered down in the padded over-the-shoulder bag she always carried. She had a large assortment of them in different colors and materials to match her outfits. It became part of her style. Wherever she went, Gypsy was sure to go. To D'Agostino, Food Emporium, Fairway, the movies, restaurants, the theatre, on buses, museums. "No Pets Allowed" did not refer to Gypsy. She was a person. She would nestle down in her carrier so she couldn't be seen and never, never made a sound, even though the top zipper was opened ever so slightly so she could breathe. Having Gypsy's warmth against her hip would have been such a comfort.

It certainly wasn't worth an argument with these two strange men who were her older sons. They had always been closer to Wally. Christian, the oldest (now twenty-five) looked very much like Wally had when she met him. The same forceful expression, unruly, thick blond hair, and cornflower blue eyes with long dark lashes. He was not as rugged as Wally, but then he had some of her blood in him, too. Wally was pure, solid Viking stock that had gotten more diluted with each successive son. Frederick had her dark hair and Johnny was definitely gened by her side of the family.

The boys had always called her by her first name. "Mother" was too formal and she certainly wasn't one of those apple pie Moms. No, "Betsy" was best. When Christian was annoyed with her, he would call her "Elizabeth" and sometimes Johnny called her "Bitsy" because she was so tiny. It was hard to believe that these great muscled bodies had been grown in her tiny womb. Physically, everything about her was diminutive. With her wavy, dark brown hair that she'd always worn long, half-way down her back, her small pointed face, translucent skin and dark saucer eyes, she seemed to be a Rossetti masterpiece. Painted by Dante Gabriel, poemed by Christina.

It was the first time she'd seen the three of them together in a long time. When the split had become a reality, ten years ago, the older boys were away at school and opted to spend their vacations with Wally. Johnny had always stayed by her side. Her protector. Her little man. Standing together, the California "twins" with their tanned faces and surfer stances looked like great Gods of the Sea. Wally would be proud of *all* of them. A wall of Krogs. Stalwart. Brave. As one they would face the enemy. And forgive whoever it was who had ended Waldemar's life, returning his soul to Odin.

"Should we stay here in the anteroom or wait in there with Wally?" Betsy whispered to Christian.

"Whichever," he said shrugging his massive shoulders. "Did you invite the cop?"

"I did speak to Mr. Kelley personally. He's not really a cop. He was just reinstated as a homicide detective because the net-work—"

"I know! I know!" He cut her off.

The tears started to well in her large brown eyes. She turned away from him toward Johnny. "Why your brother has to be so rude at a time like this," she said, her voice quavering.

"It's his way of being upset. Don't let him get to you. Remember, he was the Number One Son and he really loved him. I hear someone coming. Chin up, Bitsy."

She rewarded him with a wan smile and turned to the door, standing straight. She had invited some of the Network people and those actors and writers she had met during the six months that Wally had been on the show. She also invited their lawyer and his secretary and their accountant. They really didn't have many old friends that were in New York who might care to pay their last respects. And, under the circumstances, she wasn't sure what was the correct procedure. Johnny had taken care of those people he felt it would be proper to ask. He would be her guide. Let the audience arrive.

The first person to appear was a model-handsome, well-built man with grey hair. Johnny gave an imperceptible don't-know shrug. The man walked directly to Betsy. "Mrs. Krog, I am sorry we have to meet under these conditions. I'm Clovis Kelley." He had a rich, deep voice and such a gentle, well-bred manner. Polite.

"Thank you for coming, Mr. Kelley. And these are our sons. Christian, Frederick and John." Her voice took on its usual fluttery quality. He shook hands with the boys, acknowledging each with a slight inclination of his head. He then turned back to Betsy. "Thank you for your call. I came a little early hoping to have a few words with you. However, I think it might be easier for you if we did talk at some other time. And place." How thoughtful. Or had he read the panic in her eyes?

"Thank you so much, Mr. Kelley. I hadn't realized how much of an ordeal this was going to be for me. I'm not used to meeting so many people. Had you known Wally—before?"

"Yes," he answered and then the gentleman in him forced him to add, "I had the privilege."

"Then you must have met Johnny," she linked her arm through John's. "Wally insisted that he work on the show and I thought it was a wonderful opportunity for him to get to know his father. And to learn." The breathy enthusiasm of the phone call returned and she became animated in a most girlish way.

"I can't say I ever met John before," said Clovis looking at the tall, slender boy who had stayed beside her while the other sons had wandered into the coffin room. But he had heard of him. The trick fate played on Wally by giving him a gay son. Wally made it very clear that he was going to straighten him out "or die trying." That had been the phrase he used.

"When would it be convenient for you to meet with me, Mrs. Krog?" Clovis asked.

She looked to Johnny. "The funeral will be first thing tomorrow," he told her.

"Tomorrow afternoon?" Clovis suggested.

"Why don't you come to my apartment. I don't believe there will be any interruptions," she said, offering him her hand again. He almost expected her to curtsy.

"Here they come," said Johnny. "I'll get the boys."

Again they were lined up as the march of the mourners began. Clovis went into the inner toom to look at Wally in his pink velvet-tufted coffin made of oak with brass handles. He wondered if it was on loan or if they had really spent that much on an overnight resting place that would be fed to the flames in the morning. He knew that it was Wally's wish to be cremated and have his ashes returned to Scandinavian soil. Christian was the one designated to carry him to Aunt Inga in Viking Land.

Strains of Muzaked Mendelssohn mingled with the introductions and greetings. Betsy's high, fluted voice cut through the general underlying hushed hubbub of voices. Clovis stationed himself against the dark draped wall in the inner room with a view of the Krogs in the outer room. He could watch the arrivals and also see the invited as they entered the inner sanctum to look down at Wally, spotlit. A slight benign smile on his face. Most of the arrivals came directly from the Studio and made appropriate mumbled apologies about their appearance. Betsy, warming to her hostess role, made them feel quite comfortable. "So happy to meet you." "Wally spoke so highly of you." "So sorry we could not have met before this unhappy occasion."

Maud Sterling asked if there would be a memorial. Johnny answered by saying they would announce one at a future date. Maud, done to the nines in a black velvet mid-calf dress with black lace yolk, sported diamonds at the neck and ears. She stood with Betsy greeting the others as if she were at a supper club and preparing to sing. Allie Jones came directly up to Clovis, grasped his hand and told him how relieved she was now that he was part of their team. She then went to look upon Wally and found a handkerchief within the layers of her clothes and dabbed her eyes. Marti Livorski nodded at Clovis and then circled the coffin before looking into it. She seemed to shake her head and left.

Clovis watched as Chuck Rosen, the Director, paid homage to Betsy, then headed toward the inner room, looked around, thought no one was watching him and high tailed it out without a glance at Wally. The office staff, (including Barbie) led by Gina Serpente, the Coordinating Producer, went quickly around the coffin looking fearful as if they expected Wally to rise up and grab them. A few made one-finger crosses in deference to their inbred Catholicism. Clovis thought they looked like ducklings following Mama and wondered where Nora Easton was. Then came Max Arden, who stared for a long time down at Wally and then, with a quick turn of his chin upward, seemed to gather an invisible Shakespearean cloak and exited. An attractive grey-haired woman who Clovis knew to be Maggie List—she of the knitting needles —dressed in black, stared long at Wally. She seemed about to speak to him, shook her head and walked briskly out.

Victoria Jessup, swathed in black leather, and Wanda Lou Bergstrom, still wearing her mismatched outfit, arrived together. As Wanda Lou looked down at Wally it seemed as if she might tear up. She didn't. Vickie clenched and unclenched her jaw while looking at Wally. Then came the show stopper. Jolie Dornya as the tragic mask of Edith Piaf. Mark Golden was literally supporting her as she gathered the courage to look at the dead man. Clovis almost held his breath, expecting to hear a crescendo moan worthy of Medea. Mark guided her to one of the straight-back gold and velvet chairs that lined the room. She seemed to gulp several times before resting her head against Mark's shoulder. Poor bitch, thought Clovis, she may really have had some honest feeling for him.

And where the hell was Yancey? A few official types in suits and ties walked business-like around the coffin. Executives? Lawyers? He would examine the log book at a later time. Obviously they were there to be counted rather than for any social or emotional reason. An extremely handsome blond woman seemed to be with an erect, dour, Basset Hound of a man. She hardly looked at the coffin, more interested in the swells of drama emanating from Jolie. The man barely glanced at the corpse and took a firm grip on the woman's arm to propel her out of the room. Right after them came Matilda Listman Ryan with her face set at sympathy. After a long communion with Wally, she marched stoney-faced from the room. Two young blue-jeaned actors, holding hands fiercely, leaned against each other as they got the courage to look at the body.

Finally! Yancey, hair swept up, black sheath as advertised, went directly to Johnny and gave him a great hug. She then acknowledged Betsy and went for a last look at Wally. She stared at him longer than Clovis felt necessary. Then she came to Clovis and asked, "Do you have to stay or can we blow this joint?"

"I gather that none of the crew was invited," Clovis said.

"No. I just checked that with Johnny. And, I know I'm late but I didn't want to get in your way," she said reaching for his right hand as it snuck up to scratch his cheek.

"And if I believe that, there's a bridge down at the end of Manhattan Island that you are going to sell me for five dollars," he said, putting his arm around her.

"Ten dollars. Where you been?" She burrowed into him.

"I think we should blow this joint," he said. "What do you want to do first?"

"Eat," she smiled.

Victoria Jessup paused at the landing of the wide beige carpeted mirror-lined steps leading to the restaurant. She finger-corrected a curl in her white hair, wet her lips and made a faint moue. The mauve tint of the mirrors and dim lights made her deep suntan look sallow. Lighting was everything, she smiled at herself. In this black leather Valentino, she looked fucking chic. That was fucking, like in f-u-c-k-i-n-g. She turned and went down the remaining steps and pushed the glass door into the restaurant.

The Maitre d' headed right to her. "Madame Jessup, Madame Ryan said you would be joining her."

"Thank you, Charles," she murmured in her huskiest tone and followed him. She wondered if he honestly remembered her. It was over eight months since she'd dined with Tillie. More likely, Tillie had told him confidentially, "You will recognize her. She's quite tall and has short cropped white hair." And he would have said, "Oui, Madame," as she slipped him the obligatory five spot.

To the right of the double door of the large "in" room, Tillie was at her usual banquette nursing her usual glass of white wine. Tillie bestowed her wide Chesire grin upon Vickie as she slid into the banquette (thankful that leather could slide) and they tapped cheeks in the ceremonial face dance.

"I'm so delighted you were able to have dinner with me tonight. I realize what an imposition it must be after your first day back. You must be exhausted. What will you have?"

Vickie wanted to say a triple Wild Turkey on the rocks but experience had taught her to say, "A Campari with lots of soda, please. It was a long day but it was also envigorating. Exhilarating. It felt so good to be back in harness. I'm only sorry it happened because of Wally's—demise."

Tillie's eyes, complimented by the reflecting blue eyeshadow and mascared lashes, were wide with interest. "I can't get over how lucky it was that you were not only in town, but in the Studio yesterday. Vickie, you literally saved our asses. And I wanted to welcome you back. Salut!" she said, raising her glass as Vickie's drink arrived.

Welcome me back? That's as good an excuse as anything else. Tillie never made a move that wasn't calculated, that wasn't a set-up for some game plan she wanted to set in motion. Okay, I'll send this up the flagpole and see if she salutes. Vickie said, "The show would have been all right. After all, I did leave a well organized group that knew what was expected of them. It's a shame that Wally didn't have a chance to get things working his way."

Tillie's thin, well-manicured hand tapped her arm twice. "Oh, he did, my dear, he did. All the show meant to Wally was being paid to have all the wine and women that time would allow. He had things working his way, all right! Unfortunately, his way collided with the UBS budget. His need for sleeping in strange beds led to the creation of many unnecessary remotes. Where, I'm sure, there were strange people in those strange beds," she added impishly.

Vickie allowed herself a smile. "I did hear rumors. This is a small business, as we both know."

"Indeed." Tillie gave a throaty laugh. "That's why I'm sure you've heard the rumors of why Wally was hired."

Vickie raised an eyebrow and nodded. You go first, she thought. I'm not going to be the one to be caught with my rumors down. Stay in neutral. "They were all over town. And the Coast as well." She shook her head, negatively, knowingly.

"As you know, Vickie, I always thought you did a wonderful job with a very difficult show. And why Allie thought that Wally could improve upon it, only proves what a poor executive she is. One should never allow one's personal feeling to interfere with business decisions."

"That's the sort of thing that gives 'Show Biz' a bad name," Vickie said. Nailed you, she thought. Yes, there had been rumors. Some reflected on Vickie, herself. But others ran the gamut from the "Star" to Allie Jones to Matilda Listman, herself. Curiouser and curiouser.

"It must be getting late for you, shall we order?" asked Tillie, handing Vickie the oversize menu.

"You mean, you eat?" asked Vickie, jokingly. "You know I've always said that you are the living proof that one cannot be too rich or too thin."

"Or too suntanned, what about you?" Tillie laughed again. "What have you been doing in the past—how many months is it?"

"Six," Vickie answered. "First I went back to California to reinforce my tan at the Springs and see my relatives. And then my agent made some wonderful connections for me in L.A. and I have an assortment of things in development. But, you know, Maggie, it takes forever."

"Tell me. It took three years for me to get KEY on the air and it hasn't been easy keeping it there for these past fifteen. That's why I'm so relieved that you are back at the helm. And you must promise me," and she leaned toward Vickie, semi-closing her huge eyes, "this is just between the two of us. If you have any problems that seem to stem from the Network, you will come directly to me."

"Thank you, Tillie," Vickie said, her voice dropping even lower, "thank you for your confidence. I think you know how much I love THE KEY TO LIFE. It had become for me, a way of life. And I missed it."

Tillie patted her hand. "Ten years is a long time to be running a show. It becomes part of you. Hard to let go." She pulled back from Vickie and looked at her carefully. "That's a wonderful outfit. Ferre?"

"No. Valentino."

"Stunning. I wish I could wear bold clothes the way you do. Maybe I am too thin!" A true guffaw this time. Her eyes darted around the room and then she whispered to Vickie. "Who dunnit?"

"Done it?"

"No. D-U-N like in murder. Have you any thoughts who sent Wally back to his Maker?" Tillie's broad, flat face broke into a huge paroxysm of laughter. "The implications of that remark. Oh!" Tears of laughter spilled down her cheeks and she daubed at them with her napkin. "Sorry. It's the first real release I've had."

Vickie realized that she had forgotten how earthy and basic Tillie really could be. Peasant stock refined. When the laughter was under control, Vickie said, "I haven't the vaguest notion who could have done away with Wally. I've had so little contact with the Studio, I'm not sure how anyone felt about him." And that's my white lie for tonight.

"I certainly don't envy that Mr. Kelley sorting through the suspects," said Tillie.

"I think I may have figured out a logic that might answer the whole problem. As you know, in theatre or television or in film when anything goes wrong, there is always the one area to blame. You know."

Tillie thought for a moment and smiled. "Costumes?"

Vickie nodded. "Whenever anything goes wrong from budget on up and down, it's always costumes that get blamed and changed! So, obviously, Costumes dunnit!"

"If I knew you wanted Chinese, we could have ordered in from that place near me that you like," Yancey said as they settled opposite each other in a platformed booth at the rear of Shun Lee West.

"Come on! The way you've put yourself together tonight, you just announce Restaurant," said Clovis.

"But, darling, I dressed for Petrossian. And you're full of it. Truth?"

"I didn't want any distractions that I couldn't handle," he smiled, putting his right hand under the pink tablecloth to arrest her foot moving slowly up his pantleg. "Seriously, I would like your help. You've been very careful about keeping your work problems away from me."

"I'm glad you noticed," she smiled. "That's another reason why I love you. I'm sure you had enough input on 'the biz' with all those long-legged blue-eyed blond California look-alikes you seem to be partial to. So, as a short-legged blue-eyed blond Texan, I wanted to be—different." She put up her hand to stop him from saying anything. "Okay! Okay! So I'm still a little insecure. I did give you full barrels, though, about Wally."

"So you're a little bit human," and he reached across the table to take her hand. They looked at each other and finally Clovis turned his head. "This is the reason I wanted to come to a nice impersonal place. I need your insights on certain people. It would be invaluable. Question, why did you look at Wally for such a long time at the funeral parlor?"

"I guess I just wanted to make sure he was dead. I know that's not nice but he almost succeeded in destroying whatever self-confidence I had as an actor, as an artist. Thanks to you, even if he were right, I realized that there was more to being alive than striving for recognition, for perfecting my craft."

As the waiter hovered with the menus, Clovis ordered his Absolut and on Yancey's nod, a white wine for her. "And an extra glass of rocks." And then he told her about Wally's proposition that he'd blocked until this afternoon. "That would have been my motive for murdering him. Don't dwell on it. It's over. Now help me. Motivations. Stories. Anything you may think could be a way of arriving at some summation of Wally haters."

"First," she said as the drinks arrived, "To us."

"To us." he echoed and they clinked. "There were a few people who were noticeable by their absence. Nora Easton, Jeff R. Landon and the "Star" and husband, Tracy George, etcetera."

"As far as Ms. "Star" is concerned, her husband would have kept any form of 'ugliness' away from her. Jeff, I think, didn't show because he is not a hypocrite and most likely he just went out and got so bombed he forgot about the whole thing. Possibly Nora didn't show because she felt that there was no longer any way he could help her. On the other hand, she would want to make points with Allie Jones. Tracy has a long trip home to Jersey and I think—no, she is on tomorrow's show because I have a scene with her. She's been very tired lately. I suspect she's pregnant. You know, my love, I will tell you all that I can. But, the person for you to connect with is Wanda Lou. The Ditz herself. She's mother confessor to the new young actors, guide, advisor, teacher. The rest of us give her the stature of psychiatrist. And she is, you'll pardon the expression, like the grave. You go into her and spill your unsavory guts on her desk and she quickly makes a little gesture with her hand at her lips." Yancey demonstrated how Wanda Lou made her famous lip-locking gesture.

Since Wally had only been on KEY for six months, it might have been someone from his past. He had a checkered career. Were there any of the people currently connected with the show who had known him before? Actors? Crew? Writers? Production people? Network? As far as Yancey knew, Wally had been a first time experience for almost everyone. Certainly, Allie Jones must have been misinformed or in a trance when she hired him to replace Vickie. Vickie was okay but, after ten years, Tillie had demanded a stronger 'hand at the helm.' As creator, Tillie had a lot to say and had a direct line to Patrick. She was responsible for the writing package. She had hired all the dialoguers, outline writers and, of course, head writer, Dewey Dakin. Nobody understood what Tillie saw in him. True, he was wonderfully organized but he was always negative because he didn't have a creative bone in his body and did not know how to generate fresh material or do fixes when problems arose. No, she knew nothing about the Marti-Nora feud as she stayed as far away from the politics of the show as possible. They were two sides of the same coin as far as Yancey was concerned. Wally's family? She loved Johnny who Wally humiliated whenever possible. He was a bright, nice kid who wanted to be an actor and not a go-fer for his father. Betsy? Weird. She'd love to have *that* relationship explained to her. Everyone within distance knew about Wally's affair with Jolie. But only Jolie took it seriously. And, Wally never stopped. Satyr complex? It was a neurotic, adolescent need to pursue any female. It proved his masculinity, which might be one reason he was so hard on Johnny. Basically, he didn't like women and thought of most of them as available whores—except for darling Betsy, the best shield a man ever had.

"You know," Clovis said, "the more you talk, the more I am aware of an odd pattern. The man had to challenge anyone with something that didn't seem possible. But challenge. Put himself on top."

"The challenge became more important than the accomplishment?" Yancey asked.

"Yes. And I think that's why I made him so angry when I didn't call his bluff when he accosted me about you. It was a two-edged bluff. Part One was to prove I cared about you. Part Two was to prove how important I could be. I flunked bluff." He smiled and leaned across the table to kiss her on her forehead.

"Well, sir, Mr. Kelley, I'm surprised at this forward behaviour in public."

"You taught me. But also he—"

"I thought you weren't going to *dwell on it. It's over.*"

"It is, truly. But there is one part I'm sorry I didn't *challenge* him about. That asshole tried to tell me that he could do a three-car location scene, including water rescues—I won't bore you with the details—in a few hours. Thinking about it, now, I realize that he was stupid enough to think he could. The King." He motioned the waiter for a drink refill.

"I'm astonished. But pleased that some Wally anger is experienced by you as well as the rest of the world," she laughed.

"Except, so far, Marti and Nora and Betsy. I am looking forward to my meeting with Mrs. Krog tomorrow. And Jolie. I'm sure there are some other pro people."

The waiter brought the drinks. "Mr. Kelley?"

"Yes," Clovis answered.

"There is a phone call for you at desk. In the front."

"Thank you," Clovis said, getting out of the booth.

"But how?" Yancey asked.

"A working detective leaves signals on his answering machine. I'll be right back."

She watched him walk away. How did I get so lucky, she asked herself. No, dammit. It wasn't luck. She deserved it after all the false starts with false and other people. She closed her eyes and prayed that everything would be all right with them. She had not prayed for a very long time. A year? Could be. And what an odd place to ask God to hear her. In the middle of New York, in the dark booth of a Chinese restaurant with a huge pink dragon floating, hanging overhead. She reassured herself by remembering Her God had listened to her in places much odder than this.

"Yancey," Clovis called and she opened her eyes. He was real. "Brace yourself."

"What's wrong?" she asked as he waved for the check.

"There's been another death. Can't say murder because it looks like an accident at the moment."

"Who?" She could feel her heart throbbing against her rib cage.

"Nora," Clovis answered. "Nora Easton. Her body was found on the landing of the back staircase at the Studio about twenty minutes ago."

# Chapter 7

"I don't know how late I'll be and you work tomorrow," said Clovis as he hailed a taxi for Yancey, "so I'll stay at my pad tonight."

"Some 'pad'," she said as she kissed him. A duplex garden apartment in the four-story brownstone he owned on East 62nd Street. "Take care, my darling. I don't like to be surrounded by all this high-voltage drama." She shuddered.

"Neither do I." Another kiss. He opened the cab door for her and leaned in to the driver. "Columbus and 81st. Drive carefully."

At Studio Three Clovis was greeted by a squarish, young, unshaven man in khaki pants and shirt. "Mr. Kelley, I'm the Night Studio Manager, Mumble Mumble. I've had the back staircase declared off-limits and taped until you got here." He walked at a brisk pace through the hall leading to it. "When the body was found, I called the police immediately and Detective," he consulted the top sheet of many on the clipboard he carried, "Herbert Kaufman said the case was all yours." Efficient Mr. Mumble Mumble looked like a thousand others of the same name with the same job. He suddenly stopped short, almost causing Clovis to bump into him. "You know what? Then he laughed and said to tell you he wished you luck but didn't think you'd need it. He said he was sending the Medical Examiner and Photographer but nobody was to touch anything until you got here."

There was no door to the back staircase. It opened directly onto the hall of the first floor. Tape had been run across its width

from wall to bannister with a crudely made sign reading "OFF
LIMITS." Clovis broke the tape and walked up the seven steps of
the battleship-grey stairs with their dark rubber edging. The landing turned right. Nora Easton's body lay crumpled on her left side
in an almost fetal position, her overpermed light-brown hair press-
ing against the knees of her green whipcord slacks. The green and
plaid shirt was still neatly tucked into the slacks. Both sensible
dark green leather shoes were still on her feet. Odd. She obviously
had made no effort to break her fall. Prim in life, conservative in
death. The only clue to the fall were the loose pages from her
leather spring binder scattered down the ten steps from the top of
the staircase. She could have been struck, shot, stabbed, blud-
geoned, pushed. Or did she just fall? Why?

Accident? Suicide? Murder? No wonder she didn't show up at
the funeral parlor, thought Clovis, as he examined the body and
the area. She was preparing for her own funeral. "Gentlemen!" He
greeted the Police team that had arrived. "Do me a favor and dust
the leather binder." It was vertically balanced on the top step.
"And I want all those papers when you're through shooting. She's
all yours," he said with a deep sigh. It had been a lot easier to to
work on faked film deaths. Poor over-eager woman, where would
all her busy-ness go? "Has her husband been informed?" Clovis
asked the Studio Manager as they walked down the hall to let the
team go to work.

"Yes," said Mr. Efficient, "I called him. They live in Jersey so he
decided to go directly to the morgue, which is where Detective
Kaufman said they were going to take the body."

"Who found the body?" asked Clovis, leaning against one of the
carpeted walls.

"One of the stage hands. After the show stops shooting and the
engineers go home, there is almost no traffic on the back staircase.
Usually just me going up and down to my office. Tonight they
finished shooting at 7:30. The Studio cleared out and I went to
the Scene Dock to start my night's work." Noting Clovis' quizzical

look, he explained, "Every night we strike the sets that are not needed the next day and ship them out. And we ship in and set up the sets that are needed for tomorrow. I've got to check them in and out as well as props—furniture." He tapped his clipboard. "Once the sets are up, the lighting crews go to work and the stage hands fill in the furniture, hang the pictures and like that. So when the director comes in tomorrow at seven, the sets are up and the lighting roughed in. Then he starts moving the furniture and lighting starts refining. Then I leave and the Daytime Studio Manager takes over. We exchange notes and I go home and sleep." A wide yawn. "Actually, they're usually done by three or four ayem and the stage hands go to sleep on the furniture. I catch some shut-eye in my office."

"Who found the body?" Clovis asked again.

"Old stage hand. Moe Chernin."

"Oh yes, I'm familiar with Mr. Chernin. Got something of a chip on his old shoulder?" Clovis commented.

"You know all our secrets already, Mr. Kelley," laughed Mr. Mumble Mumble. "Moe likes to sneak away when the work gets too heavy. He creeps up the back stairs and heads for the Actors' Lounge to see what nosh may be left over. Danish, yoghurt, fruit. He eats it so 'don't go to waste.' Then he goes to sleep on one of the couches. There's no point in trying to change him or report him. He screams UNION and seniority. If you try to talk to him, he claims he's being discriminated against because he's a Jew. I hope that soon he'll plant that grove of trees in Israel. He's been threatening to do it and then retire there. But with the all the turmoil, who knows?"

"Thank you. Where can I find Moe now?"

"Some sofa on the set. He seems to favor the one in the Sheraton Library because it's longer. I'll be on the Scene Dock and then in my office if you need me," said Mumble Mumble, yawning, and left.

Clovis walked through the double doors into the Studio. As

suggested, Moe was stretched out full length on the velvet sofa in the Sheraton Library. Clovis stared down at the snoring old man, a slight smile reinforced his Alfred E. Neuman resemblance. Dreaming of trees in Israel? Or of Nora? "Mr. Chernin."

Moe's large arthritic hands knuckled the sleep out of his eyes and he slowly swung his legs off the sofa and sat up. "Who wants Moe?" The eyes opened. "Oh, it's you, the detective. So you want to know that yes I found her. I was going up the stairs to look for the Studio Manager. I wanted to know which curtains they wanted for the kid—what's her-name's bedroom."

"Do you remember what time it was?" Clovis asked, sitting down beside him on the uncomfortable sofa.

Moe's hands opened, palms up. He raised and lowered them as if weighing the air. "Time! Time. Who knows from time. When you got to do something, you do it. See over there," he pointed to the back walls of the studio where a selection of window coverings in all materials, sizes and colors were hung. "They're flown so I have to know which one to bring down for the bedroom so I go to find the Studio Manager. And there's that dumb *shickser* lying on the landing. So I tell the Studio Manager and come back here to work."

"You knew Nora Easton?"

"Nah, I don't know her." His whiney voice rose higher. "I see her around. I see all of them around. She's like a school teacher, that one. Every sentence starts with 'don't'. 'Don't sit on the furniture.' 'Don't talk during rehearsal.' Don't. Don't." He shrugged.

"Thanks a lot, Mr. Chernin," said Clovis, getting up. "If you think of anything else you want to tell me, I'll be around tomorrow."

"So what's to tell. I'm not going nowhere. Maybe I see you, maybe I don't." Placing his large hands under his knee, he lifted one leg, then the other onto the sofa. With a deep sigh, he closed his eyes and soon seemed to be asleep again.

Clovis found himself tiptoeing so as not to disturb the old man. The yawning Studio Manager smiled at Clovis. He handed him a manila envelope. "Here are the papers from Nora's binder. I have to get to work. It's midnight."

"Did you know Wally Krog?" Clovis asked him.

"I knew who he was but he never paid any attention to us lowly drones. And, he was usually out of the Studio by the time I came on duty. Sorry." as he yawned again. There was something familiar about the man. An unshaven owl. The yawn broadened his face.

"What did you say your name was?" Clovis asked.

"Michael Ryan," Mumble Mumble answered.

That was it. "Any relation to Ms. Matilda?"

"I'm her son," Michael told him. "I don't know what I want to be when I grow up and this pays the rent. Say hello to my mother when you see her," he tried to stifle another yawn.

"Go for it." yawned Clovis, as he headed out of the studio. In his gut, he knew that Nora's death was an outcropping of Wally's murder. He hoped it would be the last.

"Shit! It's all shit!" Dewey Dakin snapped angrily as he thumbed the channel changer of the TV remote. Seated on the front edge of the king-size bed, he watched the images shift.

"Darling," called his wife, in the bed, shoulders against the Windsong covered headboard. "Darling?" DeeDee repeated to his back, trying to get his attention. "Are you just hunting or are you looking for something specific? Press Mute if you're just hunting. You're making it very difficult for me to read with all that confusion." She peered at him over her gold-rimmed granny glasses— her one concession to ageing. "You *must* read this book. He hates everyone. Just like you."

"You know I don't have time to read," he growled.

"You might as well read as play with that stupid thing. Come to bed. Or if you insist on watching television, go into the den where you won't disturb me. It's after midnight."

"Oh, the hell with it." He punched the Off button and watched the screen grow dark.

She put the heavy book down and pulled up the strap of her silver silk Montenapoleone night gown to emphasize her well proportioned breasts. "Whatever is wrong with you tonight? You've been like a bear ever since you picked me up at the Studio. Neither of us *wanted* to exchange platitudes with the Krog clan but as you've told me more than once, that kind of gesture is as much a part of your job as anything else."

Pouting, Dewey removed the outer layer of his Sulka ensemble, the Foulard robe, and tossed it on the edge of the bed and watched as it slid to the floor. Nothing was working tonight. He stood at the side of the bed, a monochrome study in tragedy from his silver silk pajamas to his ashen face. Eyes and mouth pointed downward.

DeeDee knew the expression too well. She patted the Porthault sheet and pulled it down in an effort to get him to get into bed. "I'm not criticising you. Politics is a way of life in your business. You should be happy that you won't have to joust with that monstrous man any more. I must confess I'm quite happy he won't slobber over my hand and ogle my boobs." Reluctantly, he sat on the bed. "Why couldn't Tillie have dinner with us tonight?"

"She was having dinner with that dyke."

"Now, Dewey, don't start that again. I don't like your talking like that about one of my dearest friends. I would think you'd be happy that Vickie was back on the show. You, yourself, admitted that she was a hundred times easier for you than Wally. Just face the fact that you don't like producers. You *hated* that first guy—that friend of Tillie's whose name I don't even remember anymore. You leaned on her until *he* went bye-bye. Why don't you produce the show?"

Dewey clenched his hands and turned to face DeeDee, face

flushed. "Don't start with me again about that. I'm holding on as best I can. Leave me alone."

He got up and walked out of the bedroom, slamming the door behind him. DeeDee shrugged, picked up BONFIRE OF THE VANITIES and readjusting her glasses, started to read again.

Barbie buzzed Clovis on the telephone intercom. "He's here," she whispered.

"I'll be right out," he whispered back.

Eugene (Bud) Easton was hunched in one of the chairs opposite the desk in Nora's office. Faded jeans, blue work shirt, brown tweed jacket with suede elbows, shoulders drawn together, head down, thin lank hair covering his face and exposing a bald spot. Pigeon-toed, an empty corrugated carton rested against his worn Keds. He was a poster for rumpled despair.

"Mr. Easton, I'm Clovis Kelley. I do appreciate your coming by the Studio to meet with me."

Easton unfolded to a skeletal six feet and revealed a mournful Stan Laurel face. He gave Clovis a limp handshake and cleared his throat. Indicating the carton, he said in a high, monotone voice, "I had to pick up her things anyway. Do they know yet? Nora is so delicate. So fragile. She was always very careful. I can't believe it was an accident."

Clovis closed the office door. "It wasn't. She received what appears to be a Karate chop that snapped her neck. She died instantly. The fall was not what killed her."

Bud Easton's Adam's Apple bobbled a few times and he sank back into the chair. "We would have been married eleven years next Thursday. She was a good wife. Everything she did at work, she did at home. So thorough. Such an eye for detail."

"Are you in television?" Clovis questioned.

"Me? Oh, no. I'm not in the business, much too hectic for me. I teach. Nora used to be a teacher, too. We met at college. Boston U. I'm going to take her back to Massachusetts to her family. She went into research and one thing led to another. And there was so much more money in it. Truthfully, she made three times what I do. I teach Freshman English at the University. Newark, New Jersey. But she worked so hard." His awe was endearing to Clovis.

"I realize this is very difficult for you, but if I may ask you a few questions, your answers may be very helpful to us."

Easton nodded a few times and swallowed again. "Anything."

"Do you have any idea why Nora stayed late at the office after they broke last night? The taping was finished at 7:30 and, from what I have gathered, most everyone except the night crew was out of the building by 8:00. The time of her death was approximately 8:15."

"She was very conscientious, Mr. Kelley. She never would leave until she had the next day's work prepared. That's why she was so good at what she did. And, she was so thoughtful, she never liked bringing work home with her if she could help it. But she'd never complain when people called her at home with all those questions. Gosh, I would have sworn that Allie Jones was going to make Nora the Producer when Wally left the show. It was really a shame that Vickie just happened to be there. I'm sure if Vickie had been on the Coast, Allie would have given the show to Nora." He became almost animated as he talked of her. "That's all that Nora ever dreamed about. Becoming Producer. She had such good ideas for casting. And story. The whole story line about bringing Bart's mother back and nobody knowing who she was and Bart falling in love with her—that was Nora's idea. She told it to Wally and he told it to Tillie and Allie and they just loved it and are going to use it. But they thought it was Wally's idea and he never corrected them. She was kind of hurt that he didn't give her any credit but that's the kind of man he was."

"Not very scrupulous," Clovis agreed. "So you feel that she was just getting the next day in order?"

"She called me at home last night around eight o'clock. She'd always call me if she was going to be later than an hour after their

scheduled break. She told me that she'd just caught up with everything and was going to drop by the funeral parlor to pay her
respects to Mrs. Krog. Knowing Nora, chances are she was going
to stop by the Hair Room to brush and spray her hair and freshen
her make-up. The light is better in there. And on her way
down. . . ." His voice broke and he lowered his head.

"Mr. Easton," Clovis said, after a moment, allowing him to pull
himself together, "did Nora have any idea or thoughts on who
murdered Wally?" Easton shook his head negatively. "Have you
any notion how she got along with her colleagues? Allie Jones.
Tillie Ryan. Marti Livorski."

"Allie always seemed very enthusiastic about Nora's potential.
She'd always tell me what 'a fine little woman' I had. I never could
read Tillie. As for Marti, she and Nora never did get along from
the time Vickie brought her on to KEY. Marti resented Nora
because she had a college degree and could express herself well.
Also, Marti was always a bit too—I guess the polite word is
vulgar. So they clashed. I never did know why Allie put such store
in Marti. Of course, when Wally came on the show, he aggravated
the situation."

I just bet he did, thought Clovis. He wondered if Easton had
any notion of the cross currents, tugging, simmering beneath
KEY's deliberately calm public surface. "So other than Marti, as far
as you know, Nora had no personality problems with the hundreds of people on the show?"

"Believe me, Mr. Kelley," Easton said, "Everyone respected
Nora." And with a smitten look on his face, he added, "They
loved her, they really did."

She must have had something, thought Clovis, for Bud Easton,
Nora had hung the moon.

"Am I your number-one suspect?" Maggie List asked Clovis, with a
slight smile as she welcomed him to her dressing room.

What a handsome woman. Rail thin, she wore a simple black

cashmere sweater and skirt. Pearls at the throat. Pearls in the pierced ears. Her long grey hair was pulled back in a French twist. Elegant. A slight hint of pale-pink lipstick. Light-blue mascara emphasized her twinkly blue eyes. A face that easily wore its sixty-odd years worth of laugh lines and wrinkles. Classic, she had earned her face and was proud of it.

She noted his look. "No, I'm not in mourning for Wally. Nor, as he accused me of being, 'in mourning for my life' like poor Masha." She paused to see if he had gotten the reference. Bright man, she liked him. "I believe in simplifying things. Life can be very complicated if one isn't careful. So, for one thing, I always wear black. On screen and off. It's much easier to accessorize. And, for another, I like to come right to the point. No, Mr. Kelley, I did not kill Wally Krog."

It was Clovis' turn to smile. "Well, I'm glad to know that. That leaves me with only one hundred and ninety-nine suspects. Have any thoughts on the subject? No? Well, then, why don't you tell me about your famous knitting needle."

Maggie pointed to the skeins of teal-blue alpaca on her make-up shelf. The five inches of knitting was speared by two 10 inch #3 needles. "I've always liked to keep my hands busy. And, as you know, an actor's life is three parts waiting to one part working. Years ago, I started with needlepoint but how many pillows can one make in a lifetime! And impersonal. So I took up knitting. I love to make things for my friends and my family here at KEY. Sweaters, scarves, socks, gloves, hats. I've got a slew of back orders to fill! This," she said, holding up the work-in-progress, "is going to be a cardigan for Max Arden who plays my husband, Dwight, on the show. I was working on it yesterday. When we finished re-hearsal upstairs, I went down to the studio for camera blocking. I was sitting in the Sheraton Library set when I was called for the scene in Dwight's office at the bank. As anyone on the show can tell you, I'm notorious for stashing my knitting in strange places —and sometimes forgetting where it is. We all do that with scripts. If you go on any set and look in the drawers or under seat cushions, you'll find scripts from Day One," she laughed.

"So you were in the Bank set when the body was discovered?" Clovis prompted.

Maggie picked up the knitting, wound her right index finger around the wool and began working on the sweater. She never looked at it but stared directly at Clovis. "Yes. When I retrieved this knitting, it was in the piano bench of the Sheraton Library. I thought maybe Joe Savage, the Stage Manager, had put it there to get it out of the way. There was one needle missing. I didn't think anything about it until I heard how Wally died. Frankly, Mr. Kelley, I'm not sorry he's dead. He was an arrogant man. He never carried cigarettes but whenever he saw someone smoking, he'd snap his fingers and expect that person to give him a cigarette and light it for him. He liked having people jump to please him. He was mean. He caused pain to many people I love. But I do not believe in violence. I'm sorry if my knitting needle became the instrument of his death but I imagine if someone is sufficiently desperate she—or he—will chose any weapon that fits the moment. By the way, after his body was discovered, I tried to go home to walk my dog, but they wouldn't let me out of the building. Do you like animals, Mr. Kelley?"

"I love them. Especially the four-legged variety. I'm truly sorry that my life has been so erratic for the last years that I haven't been able to give one a proper home."

"I'm glad to hear you say that. I don't trust people who don't like animals." She paused for a moment, staring at her reflection in the large make-up mirror. "I learned long ago, Mr. Kelley, that it's very important to know one's limitations. I always wanted to be an actress so I could be someone other than *I* was. I knew that I would never be a star. These last fifteen years on KEY have been the happiest in my life. I really never had a family before this. One gets very possessive about one's family. I cherish it as much as

Penny, my dog. She's a yellow Labrador. Isn't she beautiful?" she asked, indicating the many pictures scotch-taped around the edges of the mirror.

Clovis looked at the array of pictures. Maggie with her hair down to her waist, her head snuggled into the flank of a beautiful large, gentle dog. Maggie with Max. Max modeling a hat with a tassel. And Penny. On her back, her side, sitting, panting and chewing a bone. A small sepia picture of a 1920's couple, their arms around each other.

"Your parents?" Clovis asked. She nodded. "You look very much like your mother."

"Thank you. She was very beautiful. She still is. They're both still alive." She stopped knitting and held it in front of her. "Poor, dear Max. He does so hate getting older. Fifteen years ago we looked like husband and wife. Or at least the same age. But with his 'alterations' I feel as if I now look more like his mother. But, as they say, snow on the roof is often an indication of a burning fire below."

"Send him up," Tillie Ryan said and hung up the house phone. Looking at herself sidewise in the mirror against the back wall of the bar, she smoothed her white Anne Klein jacket. She was glad skirts had gone up again. She *did* have great legs.

"Do you want me to stay or go?" Dewey Dakin asked, pulling himself out of the overstuffed armchair.

"Suit yourself. I just thought the time had come for Mr. Detective Kelley and I to have a talk." Chimes rang and she opened the door. "Thank you for coming over," she said with a broad smile. "I thought we'd have more privacy here. I don't believe you've met Dewey Dakin, my Head Writer. Clovis Kelley."

They shook hands. It was the dour Bassett Hound man. "I saw you last night," Clovis commented.

"Last night?" asked Dewey as he continued to stuff papers into his worn schoolbag style briefcase.

"At the funeral parlor. You were with a very handsome, tall blond woman."

Dewey turned and flashed a quick smile. "My wife, DeeDee. Dorothy. Tillie, I'll be at the office if you want me." A curt nod to Clovis and he left.

"May I offer you something to drink?" she asked, gesturing toward the bar.

"Thanks but it's too early for me." He looked around the room crowded with overstuffed chintz furniture. He decided on the sofa, which absorbed him as he sat. Leaving the length of the Tole coffee table between them, Tillie sat at the other end of the sofa.

"My son, Michael, told me abut Nora's unfortunate 'accident' at the Studio last night. Do you think it's related to Wally's death?"

"I do. But there's no proof as yet. We're continuing to call it an 'accident' so as not to alarm everyone."

"Mr. Kelley—"

"Clovis."

"Clovis. Tillie." He nodded.

"I agree. 'Murder Strikes Studio Again'. Headlines would be no help. I know the Network requested special help so you were reinstated by the police department. I don't trust the network."

"That's putting it bluntly," he said with admiration.

"I'm a realist or I wouldn't have lasted as long as I have in this cut-throat business. I am going to be honest with you. It will save us both a great deal of time. Do you have a personal stake in this investigation?"

"I don't need the money. I know Yancey didn't do it because she was with me. I'd like to solve this as quickly as possible and get back to *my* life. Does that answer you?"

"Then we are in complete agreement. I have the feeling that Allie would like to milk this drama as long as possible so she can appear to stay in the spotlight. But it is not in the best interests for KEY. I have a direct line to Patrick. Allie likes to tangle it. It is true that after ten years, I thought Vickie was burned out and not performing up to par. Allie fired her and brought Wally in. Her idea. No lay—no matter how good—is worth four rating points." She put her head back and laughed heartily. "I must admit for a very quick second I was taken in by his very palpable charm. What woman is not susceptible to flattery? But that was all he could do. The bottom line is performance and he failed miserably. The truth is that if Wally had not been murdered, he would have been fired."

"Who knew about that?" Clovis asked.

"A very select few. Patrick and me and Allie makes three. Unless she told her toady. Marti. Don't you hate people who end their names with a small egotistical 'i'. Fashionable spellings have always bored me. It's possible, though, Marti and Wally were quite close. She found him his apartment and God knows what else." She gave Clovis a knowing wink.

"Wally did not know about the fact that he was about to be fired?"

"Not unless Allie slash Marti told him. I have the feeling that if he knew he would have said something. He was one of those people who believed that everyone was interested in the most personal aspects of his life. At the drop of a drink, he would tell most anyone about his marriage. Elizabeth Simpson had been an innocent virgin sophomore at Chapel Hill and he had been a visiting director. It was the basic situation of countless novels and bad movies that she, unfortunately, had neither seen nor read. Trusting, sweet, delicate fragile child who yearned to experience LIFE so she could translate the churning within her thin, underdeveloped breast into POETRY. The very ethereal quality that had attracted him, ended up trapping him. Girls, college girls in America, were supposed to know how not to get pregnant. I think he may have fancied himself in love with the startled faun-like child. He admitted that it had been like 'fucking a bird.' She was almost half his age, nineteen going on six. He was thirty-four. She had an old world, not quite American quality that he found very appealing. He could not resist her. She claimed they were 'fated' to be married. Fated all right. If he refused, Betsy's father was going to run him out of the country. 'Moral terpitude' was the phrase her father used. So they married and when Christian was born, Wally took great pride in being a father. He liked the idea so much, he impregnated her again. Frederick is just nine months younger than Christian. He learned the expression 'Irish twins.' But Betsy continued to be the child-bride and he wanted a woman. And so started the dalliances while she played with her live dolls. He would have left her, I believe, but the marriage was a convenience that protected him from committing to anyone else. Oh yes, and there was Johnny three years after Frederick. All I can say, it's a lucky thing, he never had daughters." Tilly broke into gales of laughter. She laughed until tears streamed down her cheeks. "I'm sorry, it really isn't funny. It's perverted. But Wally with a *daughter.*" She brushed the tears from her cheeks. "Incest. The one real taboo on television."

"Is that why everything about the workings of television is so incestuous?" Clovis commented.

"Yes," she agreed. "I guess it is. It's the nature of the beast. Cross-pollination. Great Mafia families intermarrying. An exclusive club but once you have your passport, you can travel from show to show. 'Show Biz,' as I'm sure you've seen, is based on the Peter Principal of failing upward. It's like politics. Use whatever cliché comes to mind—one hand washing the other or those you meet on the ladder going up are the same ones you meet on the ladder going down. And all of that is especially true of Daytime because it is a much smaller world."

"This is my first brush with the Daytime world," said Clovis. It's really very different than nighttime. Or Prime Time as they like to call it."

"Well, for one thing, Daytime pays Nighttime's bills. But, I like it because from a storytelling point of view I can do much more.

There isn't a story I cannot tell. It is the great continuing story line that started with the cavedwellers to the mesmerizers of Ancient Greece to Scherherazade. Dickens. Why the Bible is the greatest book of source material in the world. The only things that change are the names and the mores. I almost forgot Shakespeare. Take any of his plots, give it a spin and I'm in business."

"Obviously, you like what you do and won't let anything stand in its way."

"Oh," she admitted, "I have a busy life. I've raised five children. And now have three grandchildren. Good peasant stock, Clovis. The best kind!"

"Is Michael your youngest?"

"There's one younger who is at home in Pennsylvania with my husband. But Michael is my wild one. He's getting to be too old to be untamed. One shouldn't have a favorite child and I don't. But I can tell you, that under that laid back, efficient cover, a wild man rages in there. He's most like me of all my children." She stood up. "What can I do for you to help you get back to your life?"

"Keep a direct line to me, too," said Clovis as he got up to go. He handed her a card with his number on it. "As a story teller, you'll know what I need filled in. Thank you."

Tillie walked him to the door. "Yancey's finally hit pay dirt. If you do her wrong, you'll have me to answer to." She kissed his cheek. "When my husband comes to town, we should all get together. Believe me, I don't say that often. As he says, he prefers to shovel snow in Pennsylvania than shovel shit in New York."

Betsy Simpson Krog lived in a sturdy pre-WWII apartment house on 85th Street between Broadway and West End Avenue. Manned by a sullen Hispanic in an ill-fitting blue with once-gold-braid uniform and cap, he told Clovis that Mrs. Simpson lived in Apartment 2F. He made no effort to announce the visitor and pointed to the self-service elevator.

Pausing outside 2F, Clovis heard strains of a Chopin Etude being played erratically on the piano. As he pushed the bell, the playing stopped and the barking began. After a long wait (was she playing the piano naked and changing into something appropriate?) Betsy opened the door with a flourish, holding a tiny growling fur with a black bow in its top knot and wearing a black rhinestone-studded collar.

"Sorry to keep you waiting, Clovis. This is Mr. Kelley, Gypsy. (Growl. Growl.) He's the man I told you who is going to work on Daddy's death. Please, please come in." She held the door for him and he walked into the dark, lamp-lit living room. A baby grand Steinway, covered with a Spanish shawl, stood by a bank of semi-closed beige wood Venetian Blinds through which an inner court-yard and facing apartment could be seen. There was a European feeling to the room. The large mahogany furniture upholstered in somber, muted colors had the heirloom look of a forgotten legacy. Two dark velvet wingbacked chairs flanked a round table smoth-ered with photographs in as many style frames as could be found in an "Exposures" catalogue. Betsy seated herself in one of the chairs, the dog tucked next to her. She sat ankles crossed, hands folded in lap. In her navy blue Laura Ashley (with matching velvet ribbon in her long brown hair) with its white lace collar and her Mary Jane shoes, she looked like a turn-of-the-century child wait-ing for *her* photograph to be taken.

"I'm sorry I took so long to answer the door," she said in her fluttery voice. "I made notes yesterday about what I was going to tell you but then I've lost them. I can't find them anywhere. That used to get Wally so angry. He'd ask me to write out story lines for him and I would always mislay them. I'm a writer." Said as a fact.

"Novels, plays, poetry, screenplays?" Clovis asked.

"I've had some poetry published in small journals that I'm sure you've never heard of," said with a lilting laugh. "A few little plays have had readings way off-off Broadway. I'm not what you might call a 'commercial' writer. But Wally loved to pick my brain for ideas and kept threatening to make me write for THE KEY TO LIFE. To earn my keep." She turned her head and looked at him, her large brown eyes unblinking. "I think I could talk to you without reading what I'd written."

"Whatever makes you most comfortable," Clovis offered.

"From the moment I heard your voice on the phone yesterday, I just knew we would be in tune. I like the cadence of your voice. Do you sing?"

"Not even in the shower," he smiled.

"You should. I can tell. You have such a beautiful deep voice."

"I love music too much to destroy it. That was Chopin you were playing."

"Yes. I'm just learning that Étude. I play the piano and the lute, guitar and dulcimer. And, of course, the lyre." She recited each instrument like a child saying a lesson. "Lyre is the modern term for the kithara that I played as a child in Greece."

"You were born in Greece?"

"No. Minnesota." She took a deep breath. "I played the kithara in Greece in one of my earlier lives. I think it was around 520 B.C. You see, Wally and I have known each other in many other lives. That is what I wanted to tell you. Wally isn't dead." There are a lot of people who are going to be very disappointed if that's true, thought Clovis. "When we die, only our bodies die. Our souls leave the body and take astral forms. We've all experienced many incarnations from the beginning of time. Wally has always been trying to find a higher plane. A wandering star searching for his place in the Heavens. And like the Phoenix, he shall rise again and again. In some future life, he and I will join together again." She stopped and cocked her head at Clovis.

"I believe," he said quietly, "anything is possible. Each person must solve life in their way."

"I knew I would like you," she said with a slight smile. "What sign are you. Don't tell me. I know. You're a Leo."

"I can't deny it," he sighed.

"I'm a Capricorn. Poor Wally was an Aquarius. You see, there are no accidents, Clovis. Even though Wally's death is sad and untimely, there must be a reason for it. Each person knows his or her own truth. The person who caused Wally's death must have been in great pain. And still is." She closed her eyes and raised her head. Going into a trance, Clovis wondered. She lowered her head and peered up at him almost kittenishly. "Wally could be a naughty boy with the ladies. I used to tease him about his conquests. Once he had that, he'd lose interest." Hand to chest, then down to tweak the dog's ears. "I shall miss him. Didn't that pink velvet in the coffin make his white hair show nicely?"

"Yes, it did," Clovis agreed. "Tell me, Betsy, do you have any idea who killed Wally?"

"You'll find out," she said rather flirtatiously. "You always get what you want, King of the Jungle!"

This forty-six year old ageing child suddenly made him feel like a dirty old man. Wally had certainly met his match in Betsy. "Do you think it was someone connected with KEY?" Clovis persisted.

"Of course." She picked the dog up and kissed its nose. "Anyone who knew Wally for any length of time, knew he really didn't have any fangs at all. Whoever took him from this life, must have felt threatened because of their own insecurities. Wally could provoke but, just like little Gypsy, his bark was much worse than his bite."

# Chapter 8

Clovis knocked on Yancey's dressing room door, # 10. "Come in." Yancey, in a flowered robe, was being held in an embrace by a large blue-jeaned and jacketed white-haired man. "Do I say oops. Or should I come back later?" Clovis asked.

"Darling, you know Chuck Rosen, my favorite director?"

"Now look what you've done." Rosen berated Yancey in mock anger. "Thanks a bunch. You are the worst."

Yancey closed the door. Sotto voce. "Chuck wasn't sure how to approach you. He has some information that he feels might be useful to you. Would you believe that this big galoot is shy."

"You weren't supposed to tell anyone," Chuck pouted childlike.

"You can stay here. I've got to shoot the fantasy so we can roll it in later." She flashed her robe revealing a skimpy nightgown that gave a new meaning to decollete. "See you guys." She gave each a cheek kiss and started out. "Now you be nice to Chuck," she admonished Clovis, and dashed out yelling, "I'm coming. I'm coming!"

"That one does not know how great she is. Maybe that's why she is—so great," said Chuck.

"No argument," Clovis agreed. Silence. Another one. Okay. "Chuck, I understand your reluctance. But at the moment I have hardly a clue and would be very grateful—"

"This isn't easy for me. I'm not a gossip. I take in a lot. I make believe that I don't know what's going on. Wally was a piece of shit. He invaded this show like a bad disease and made everyone sick. Factions. You were with Wally or you were against him. No inbetween. He hung out with his 'team.' A couple of the actors. A few cameramen. Frank Quinn—he's the only one here bigger than I. And Lester Williams, good-looking black guy. They weren't married so they'd hang out with him. Go to the Y for push-ups and wrestling. 'You vant to ahm rassel.' Always challenging. Elbow on table, arm straight, fist raised. Kid stuff. They'd hang out in his office or that toilet they call the Engineers' Lounge. And the men's room. About a month ago, I go to the john on the second floor and into a booth. Right above the toilet paper in this big scrawl is: 'Lester sucks white—' I can't even say the word. It's got four letters and starts with 'c'. I'm trying to figure out if I should do something about getting it cleaned up when Lester comes into the john followed by Wally. Lester had seen it and wanted Wally to see it. The writing was in green. Everyone knew that Wally used only green pentels. Whether Wally did it himself or someone swiped one of his pentels, I don't know. Anyway, Wally laughed. Lester got mad. And I called the Studio Manager to get it painted out. Fun and games with Wally."

"Was there any truth in the graffitti? Was it based on some relationship at the Studio?" Clovis wondered.

"I honestly don't know. I was aware that Lester did hang out a lot with Nora. He'd go up to her office and they'd shmooze. Door was always open. Frankly, I always thought Lester was a little bent. I was sorry to hear about Nora's accident. She was a pain in the ass but she couldn't help it. Nag. Nag. Nag. Somebody had to do the work. Wally didn't. So, there it is. I hope it will make some sense to you." He got up to go and then paused. "There's something that keeps bugging me. It's on the tip of my brain. I was on the floor when Wally was killed. I had my console pointed away from the Sheraton Library. We were all concentrated on the Bank Set. But there was something . . ." He snapped his fingers. "Now I know! Wally was on the Studio floor. That was quite unusual to begin with. Then he walked in front of the cameras through the

Bank Set—anyone else would have the sense to walk behind the cameras—and he seemed to be signalling someone. Damned if I know who."

"Now all I have to do is find out who that was. As you would say, Chuck, thanks a bunch."

Left shoulder raised to cradle the telephone, right hand writing notes on a yellow legal pad, left hand searching through a stack of photocards on her desk, Wanda Lou Bergstrom stopped all activity as she saw Clovis standing in the open door of her office.

"Thanks, Tex, I'll get back to you," she said, hanging up the phone. Smiling broadly, "Come in. I wondered when you were going to get to me. Please close the door or we'll have at least three thousand interruptions." She patted at her short bronze hair with both hands. "You do know you have one of the loveliest, prettiest, brightest ladies. She's not an actor. She's a person."

"There seems to be a conspiracy around here to convince me about Yancey. I'm convinced. She says pretty okay things about you, too. Great reviews."

Wanda Lou beamed. "I've known Yancey almost from the time she came to New York. Ambitious, hard-working and talented. An unbeatable combination. But one still needs the magic of luck. Being in the right place at the right time. When the part of Sally surfaced, I had just seen Yancey in SWEET CHARITY and brought her in to audition. She was still a bit rough around the edges but I *knew* she was perfect for the role. Vickie always relied on my instinct and Allie was fine, as I remember. Dewey was the hold-out. Didn't think she was pretty enough. Tillie convinced him. Dewey measures every female against that icy wife of his."

"I saw her at the funeral parlor," said Clovis. "She is a stunner."

"Used to be a top model. She wears the pants in that family. Talk of hen-pecked. Serves him right, he's such an up-tight Southern snob. I'm always suspect of those veddy proper types. There's got to be a crack in that pillar of society. There have been a few hints that the marriage is not as perfect as it seems. I've never pursued that or any vein of gossip." She made a key locking gesture with her right hand in front of her lips. "I keep my trap shut but I can't help but absorb secrets people feel impelled to lay before me. Mostly actors, poor dears. *Sooo* insecure." A sympathetic shake of the head and her bronze curls bounced.

"Yancey says you know which closets have closets. What can you tell me that you believe might help me sort out those who truly had motives to silence him?" He made a lip-locking gesture. They both laughed.

"Ever since I saw that close-up of Wally with that thing in his neck, I've been wondering who would have the courage to do that."

"And the strength," Clovis added.

"You know, at first I thought that Wally was kidding. Another one of his very cruel jokes. He spread venom and distrust wherever he could. He made this a very unhappy place to work."

"I've picked up clues here and there about various people who frankly despised the man and are much happier with him out of the picture. But that doesn't necessarily mean they are going to put their life on the line to get rid of him. Several have come to me to tell me that they didn't kill him. Yet, I am certain that they're holding something back."

"Could you be more specific?" Wanda Lou asked.

"Jeff Landon. He told me about his agent and AIDS."

"That was typical of Wally. Poor Damon Mandel. Such a lovely man." Another sympathetic curl-bouncing head shake.

"I didn't want to push Jeff at that time but I have a feeling that there was something more that Wally had on him."

A deep sigh. "There was. There is. Before Jeff got into soaps— and he's made a profession of them—he had another profession."

"Male whore?" Clovis speculated.

"Could be. But it was something better documented. Jeff had done a great many porno flicks. Wally's tastes being what they were, I suspect that he found out about that episode in Jeff's career and tormented him about it. Most likely threatened to go to the Network and that would not sit well at all. Those millions of little girls with crushes on Jeff. And their mothers as well. Not easily forgiven in the 'Bible Belt.' It's one thing for a preacher to have a sudden flirtation with the devil and be seduced by a prostitute. But how can one explain that a grown man willingly lived by the size of his private parts over and over again?"

"A natural for Wally. Who else had a problem that Wally would have exacerbated?"

Wanda Lou thought for a moment by taking the plastic yellow butterfly comb from the back of her hair and scratching her head with it. "Yancey for one. He made her so miserable that she was ready to tell the United Broadcasting System to tear up her contract. That would have meant very serious problems for her in the future as a prima donna. A reputation for walking out on a contract does not sit well. And poor Tracy George, that lovely child. Wally couldn't keep his hands off her. She's recently pregnant and she knew Wally would get rid of her rather than let the writers use the pregnancy in her story line."

"Did he really have that much power?" asked Clovis. "Unbelievable!"

"No, he didn't but the actors thought he did. He played one against the other and the writers against the actors. Chaos. He revelled in it. Wally tormented Maxwell Arden about his fan club, threatened Maggie List because he knew she was the sole support of her ageing parents. He had just started in on Heather Leigh, our new and nubile ingenue. I try to warn the girls but they don't or won't listen. The *Producer* wants to screw them and some feel flattered, others actually still believe they can get ahead that way. Wally, the Great Convincer. I started out to be an actor but thank heaven I changed my course early on. But I'm married to one for almost twenty years and I can tell you they're a breed apart. Men, women, horses, dogs, cats—and actors." She turned to look at a large portrait head of a handsome man with heavy eyebrows, wavy hair and Gable ears. In a gold frame on the wall next to her. "That's Jeb," she explained to Clovis.

Clovis searched for something pleasant to say about him other than the obvious fact that Jeb was handsome in a very ordinary way. "He has a very kind face."

"That's his problem. He lets everyone walk all over him. Including me. Ah, well." Wanda Lou shifted gears. "I have never understood how the Network functions or why they allowed Wally such seeming latitude. They must have known how destructive he was. My guess is that he bamboozled first Allie and then Tillie. I'm sure Marti was in there somewhere. Tough ladies."

"And Nora?" asked Clovis

"So sad about her. She was always running, running but standing in the same place if you know what I mean." Clovis nodded. "She felt so guilty about the fact that she was sterile and couldn't give Bud the baby he wanted so badly. The more he suggested adopting, the later and harder she worked. Or, really, worked at working. Talk of your mountains out of molehills. Too bad, she had that accident just when Vickie came back."

"You seem to be very fond of Vickie Jessup," Clovis noted.

"She's a dear. We are old, old friends. I'm still not sure if it was Tillie or Allie who shafted her. But Vickie will make this place hum again. Actually, Vickie could tell you a lot more about the crew, the writers and that other side of the show. Vickie and DeeDee Dakin are very close. Dewey is such a fool he's even jealous of their friendship. I guess he thinks Vickie isn't 'good enough' for DeeDee," Wanda Lou laughed.

Or maybe, too good, thought Clovis.

As Clovis approached his office, Barbie stood up and signalled him elaborately. In today's selection of white on white on white, she looked like a cross between a Michelin tire ad and a Pillsbury

Dough Boy. "I couldn't stop her," Barbie whispered, "she insisted on waiting for you in there." She pointed to his office.

A small figure was perched on a chair that had been pulled up to the table on which her elbows rested. Cradling her chin in her hands, Jolie Dornya was absorbed in the runthrough of THE KEY TO LIFE on the largest of the television sets.

"You wanted to see me?" Clovis asked her.

She jumped. "Don't you ever knock?" she reprimanded him in French and then translated it into English.

"Not into my office. Shall I go out and come in again?"

"No, No," she replied without humor as he shut the door behind him. "Cette fille," she began, "that girl, she wouldn't let me smoke." She pushed her lips forward into a pout that accentuated her bird look. Parrot? Condor? She uncrossed her legs slowly and stood up to her full five feet. Faded, torn-at-the-knees blue jeans were stuffed into high-heeled black boots. An oversize pink man's shirt was knotted at the waist showing navel. She had been sitting on a large wine-colored leather Hermes combination address and date book. "Here," she said, thrusting it at him. "I came up here and stole it from him because he made me very angry. Très faché. Very mad."

Clovis took the book. On the lower corner in gold black letters was "Waldemar Krog." Opening the book, he saw that the entries were in Wally's handwriting. Green ink. "When did you take it?"

"Two days ago. The night before he was supposed to come to my apartment and he did not show up. It was not the first time. I called his phone at home. There was no answer. Not even that fucking machine. I was so," she clenched her fists and shook her small body searching for the right word, "so, so MAD I almost went up there. But something tells me no. So the next morning— it was my day to show up early by eight at the Hair Room—I come right into this office. Wally was always late. I know that he keeps that book in there," she pointed to a cabinet behind the table. "I start to look in it and then I think fuck you and I take the whole book. I knew it would upset him and also maybe I learn something. He has lots of names I know and some I don't but I figure out he keeps a record of who he fucks. Can you imagine that man?"

Unfortunately I can, thought Clovis. "How did you figure that out?"

"Because he makes tracks. He has little initials he puts circles around. Regardez!" She grabbed the book, opened it and pointed to a small "j" that had been circled. She flipped a few pages where there were similar markings. "I check my book. Those are nights he spends with me. He never lets me come to his apartment. But, look, look." She thumbed a few pages and pointed to other initials with circles around them. "Mornings. Lunch hour. Sometimes after me." She became more agitated as she illustrated the magnitude of Wally's sexual appetite. "He was not a very good lover. He was a pig, that man." She made a spitting sound with her mouth.

"Are you implying that until you went through this book you didn't know about Wally?" The question sounded more astonished than he wanted it to. This woman was on the edge and could turn rabid. To Clovis' relief, the question calmed her and she sat down again.

"First week Wally comes on the show, he sits in my chair and asks for a trim. He stares at me in the mirror the whole time. When I finish, he asks how much. I tell him it is against the union rules for me to accept money from him. He laughs and says I can take it out in trade and gives me a kiss on the cheek. So for six months everyone knows that Wally screws me. It don't hurt for everyone to know I have, as you say here, the producer's ear. They come to me for favors from him. What they don't know is that he don't listen to me. He only listens to himself. What's good for Wally. Then he tells me he wants me to fuck his fairy son. He thinks I can make Johnny a man. He says it's a compliment. I think it's an insult. So I tell him I'm through with him and this place. Then he asks me to marry him."

"Was he planning to divorce Betsy?"

"Quelle blague! He just didn't want to be responsible for the show losing the best hairdresser it's ever had. You think it's easy dealing with those actors? Bitches. Who needs it? I could be doing feature films. Commercials where they really pay money. I could open my own place. On the East side. I could go to Hollywood. I don't have to stay on this lousy daytime soap making those dogs look beautiful." The angrier she got, the thicker the accent until she was spluttering in an odd patois. She rubbed her hand through her black-roots brassy red hair and then reached into her shirt pocket and took out a pack of Marlboros. "I must smoke."

"Who do you think killed him?" She shrugged her shoulders. "Could it be someone who wanted a favor and didn't get it?" Another shrug. "Did he have any particular enemies?"

"Who killed him? He killed himself. He was much hated."

"Certainly you didn't hate him. You must have felt something to be so overcome when he died," Clovis suggested.

Knock. Barbie stuck her head in the door. "Jolie, they need you down in the Hair Room."

"Need. *Merde.* Curls are more important than dead people to them." She turned and faced Clovis. "I do not cry for him. I cry for me. I always cry at endings. No one mattered to him. I wanted him to have a broken heart. Not a stopped one. I wanted him to hurt so I could laugh at him. I wanted to—gloat. Now I can't." She started out and stopped. "When you are through with that book, can I have it? I'd like to have something of his." She didn't wait for an answer.

Clovis opened Wally's expensive date book. It was a testament to a life filled with sexual exploits and VIP activities. Mets opening. Met opening. Museum opening. No theatre. No movies. Parties. And the Y. Plus Jolie's tiny encircled "j", there was an alphabet jumble of other letters. A popular one was "m". Could be Marti Livorski as Tillie Ryan had implied. It was doubtful that a jealous lover could be so obsessed by a man of Wally's nature to destroy him. He was the kind of man who lead to fantasies of torture but the torturer would want him to know who was at the controls.

And Nora? Why Nora? Were the two murders related? Beside being a nuisance, what quality did she have that could inspire such hatred. Lester Williams, the black cameraman with whom she seemed to have a rapport? Moe Chernin, the aged stage hand who found her body? Her ever faithful and loving husband, Bud Easton —if her last night's phone call had actually taken place, it would be in the records, if not, had his devotion turned? How ignominious if her death were an error! Or did Miss Busy Body just busy her body too much?

"Hi, there!" The tone was seductively husky.

Clovis looked up to see Victoria Jessup standing just outside his office. Her office. "Hi, yourself. Come in." He stood up.

"A true gent," she smiled. Her teeth gleamed white in her tanned face. Today's monotone color was purple, which emphasized the whiteness of her short curly hair. Silk blouse, leather slacks. "I wanted to let you know we're going to need this office tomorrow morning for a special story meeting. To get me caught up, get my input. Hah!" Her voice was so hoarse that her laugh sounded like a bark. "This is the only office big enough to hold the writers' contingent, the Network contingent and me. We hold the meetings at the Studio so that the Producer is available for any emergency," she explained. "I'll miss Nora, she was a great help. But the meeting will go a lot faster."

"Why is that?" asked Clovis.

"Occasionally, Nora and Marti would get into childish squabbles that ended up sounding like 'my father can beat your father' logic. They were both right and both wrong. Nora protecting the production and Marti parroting the Network party line. The only time they seemed to get on the same wavelength was when they would take on Dewey. Mr. Didactic himself."

"Will Allie and Tillie be here tomorrow?"

"Oh yes. It's a minor miracle when we can get a meeting together. What with Tillie's beating the traffic from Pennsylvania, and Dewey's shrink and Athletic club, and Allie's staff and Status meetings, and my production meetings. I think a Summit would be easier to arrange." She looked at her watch.

"Do you have a minute more?" Clovis asked.

"They're in notes now after the runthrough. Until they're ready to tape, I can make myself free." She called, "Barbie, tell Gina I'll connect with her after taping." She turned back to Clovis. "Gina Serpente, the Coordinating Producer. She's the one who really makes this show happen. She takes all the disparate information from actors' vacations to script rewrites, crew replacements, editing changes, set alterations and coordinates it all into a comprehensive, workable schedule. Organization plus. Have you met her?"

"A tall, anorexically thin, dark-haired woman who speaks in whispers," Clovis acknowledged.

Vickie bark-laughed again. "I think she's afraid the information will vanish if it's exposed to air. She's the only person I can think of who was not upset by Wally's continual changes. She seemed to look forward to them as if she were in training for some mental Olympics so she could meet the challenge and score higher each time. Quite a wonder!"

"Was she one of your finds?"

"Not really. She was on the show when I got here ten years ago. A secretary. And she worked her way up to Coordinator which is what her job is. When Wally came on the show, she threatened to quit so he, in his largesse, dubbed her a Coordinating *Producer*. I know it pissed Nora off. They did *not* hit it off from that moment on. Poor Nora."

"Does her death surprise you?" Clovis asked.

"Only the way it happened. Nora always played fragile and invalid to a point I was almost grateful when she managed to come to work. I guess I expected that one day she would be wafted up to Heaven like Little Eva," Vickie smiled.

"Was she really ill?" Clovis asked.

"Frankly, I always thought it was up here," she touched her head with her forefinger. "Yet she had enough doctors' appointments to keep her out of the Studio more than I thought necessary. I'm told her pattern changed quite a bit when Wally arrived on the scene." She suddenly turned abruptly to face Clovis. "You don't think Nora's death had anything to do with Wally's murder?"

Clovis could answer honestly. "I don't know." He watched as her face registered shock, surprise and acceptance. "Did you stay in touch with her?"

"We had lunch a few times as I did with many of the other people who work the show. I couldn't have produced the show for ten years without making some friends. In spite of myself. And then there are some I knew long before I produced KEY. Wanda Lou. Maggie List. Others. And since I live in the neighborhood at 62nd and Broadway, I was always bumping into people who would fill me with horror stories about Wally and ask when I was coming back. Wally could find someone's Achilles heel and hammer nails into it. Like Gina. She's Italian and lives with her parents in Brooklyn. Ever since I've known her she's gone with Pasquale Giambrone—Pat. He works at the Post Office. Everyone's always known, that but Wally pounced on it and started to put her down. He'd tease her with things like 'So when does one get to meet your legendary Romeo. He's a wop, isn't he?' Or he'd ask when her Uncle Sal was going to put cement shoes on someone. Gina never answered him so his baiting got uglier. She called me in tears asking what she could do as it was beginning to interfere with her work, her pride. I told her to ignore him but I called one of his buddies, Big Frank the cameraman, and asked him to tell Wally to lay off. Frank called me back and told me he had spoken to Wally whose attitude was that he thought Gina liked it because it proved that he was aware of her. A lot of good guys on the crew. But boys will be boys, as my mother used to tell me, and they liked to play some of Wally's pig games."

"So, as far as you know, none of the stage hands or crew members had a specific grudge, ax to grind, hatred of Wally?"

Vickie thought for a moment. "You can't be a good producer and have everyone like you. I'll take respect instead of liking anytime. But Wally was not respected and was almost universally hated. His decisions, from what I've been told—and told—were not based on anything but his own whim. His own pleasure. If he didn't have anything to do in the evening, he would insist on redoing scenes over and over until all hours so he'd have something to do. Even overtime money couldn't compensate for his mindlessness. The stagehands—okay, call them gorillas," she smiled, "are a good group and have a basic loyalty to the show which they really hope is good. They don't like being ignored as *nameless* gorillas. And the engineers like to work together and not be pitted against each other and 'blamed' for equipment failure over which they have little control. Wally was totally insensitive to everyone around him. He made changes not for improvement but to prove to everyone that he was The Big Boss controlling all their lives. No, I don't think any of them would want to kill him. If they did, they would have made it look like an accident. They ain't dumb, those boys."

She seemed to be a bit more relaxed, thought Clovis. Handsome woman but her eyes did have a shifty quality. Was it the situation or something more involved? "Have you any idea how he got on with the writers?"

She thought again before answering. Had she prepared answers to question she thought he might ask her? "The only ones on the writing team he would have anything to do with were Tillie and Dewey. The head honchos. The outline writers, dialoguers and editors were beneath his notice. He would have Nora prepare his comments for the story meetings."

"Language barrier?" asked Clovis with a smile.

A quick smile back. "That man knew no barriers. He was too lazy to read the outlines and had little story sense. At first he conquered Tillie with his old, very old world charm." She raised her right hand to her lips and kissed it. "But Tillie's smarter than that, I think. He and Dewey did not hit it off at all. A bit of both jockeying to be top jock. Wally's superiority was of the put-down variety based on his idea of himself as arbiter. Dewey, however, is a bona-fide snob. Bred in the bone."

"And what's his Achilles heel?"

" 'He who steals my purse steals trash' " Vickie quoted, smiling. "His noble Southern background."

"That means his family as well," Clovis suggested. She nodded. "Kids?"

Vickie looked at her wristwatch. Why is he taking this tack with me, she wondered. He could find out about Dewey's family from anyone. What does he know? "Yes. Daughter named Holly who's thirteen and a son, Dewey Dakin III, called Beau. He's a year older."

"The perfect American package," Clovis commented. "Are they brought up in the traditions of the South?"

"Not being from the South myself, I couldn't say. But I do know he's very strict with them. Only two hours of supervised television watching a day. Proper dress. Holly can't date until she's fifteen and Dewey's been known to listen to their phone conversations and disconnect when he's not happy with the gist. He can be something of a martinet."

"And his wife, DeeDee I believe she's called, how does she feel about it?"

"I suggest you ask her," said with a polite smile as she got up and looked at her watch again. "I better go see what's taking so long. They should be through notes by now."

"Notes to actors?"

"Interpretation changes, placement rearrangements for camera, costume changes, hair touch-up. Notes from me to the director to the actors," she explained.

"Lucky for everybody you were right here," said Clovis.

"Yes," Vickie replied, flushing through her deep tan. She tousled her short cropped curly white hair. "But I still haven't been able to get the hair trim I came for. Jolie's been too upset and I've been too busy."

"Tape time. Tape time." The Stage Manager's announcement could be heard on the public address system as Vickie opened the door.

"You're welcome to join us in the Control Room" Vickie said graciously.

"Thanks. Maybe later. And thanks for the talk." He watched as she walked unhurriedly toward the back staircase. Her padded shoulders were rigid as she moved somewhat like a wind-up doll. Remnants of a dance or modelling career? There was a file in the cabinet behind him labelled "Press Releases." The usual falsified bios but usually there was enough truth to help check facts through.

The time had come to examine Ms. Victoria Jessup more closely. The hoarse ex-smoker's voice and bark-laugh gave her an aura of buddy-buddy friendliness. The chic all-leather combos had a veneer of sophistication. Yet the hooded hazel eyes were wary and uncertain. She was hiding something. She had been in the Studio when Wally was killed. Motive? Wanted her old job back? No guarantee with that Tillie/Allie team. Yet the ten years of producing KEY had given her an identity, a purpose that she obviously enjoyed.

Clovis reached into the inner pocket of his J.C. Penney's miner's jacket and pulled out a stack of 3 x 7 memos. "From the desk of Clovis Kelley". Red on white souvenirs from his consultant days on "Diary of a Cop." He shuffled through and pulled out the one headed "Jessup" neatly printed in his large vertical strokes. Owned a Condo on West 62nd Street. Lived alone. No car. No weekend house. No pets. No people. No problems? Small income from mother's estate. San Diego Bank. Graduated Stanford '59 just in time to be a Hippie. Arrived New York in the 60's to study acting at the Academy. Worked for an agent before starting into producing. Tall, tanned, athletic, humor and style. Blank! What was missing?

Who had also been at the Studio when Wally was murdered and Nora's "accident" had occurred? He knew in his gut it was the same person. The same attack, almost maniacal in fury, on both victims was too similar. In any KEY TO LIFE story line it would be the same person! Life imitating soap opera. He flipped through his stack of memos pulling out those he felt had both motive and opportunity. He had winnowed the list of two hundred down to under twenty. Most of the studio personnel didn't even know who Wally was. They had had no identity for him, easily replaceable drudges.

Vickie's name headed the "Suspects" list. As he looked at the names, he wondered if humiliation was a sufficient motive. Possibly for a psychotic. And of those he could nail at the Studio with a good reason for offing Wally, how many could he put back in place for Nora's death. Damn. Oh, for a cigarette. A few more questions to some unlikely people and a few answers from unlikely places and he'd be able to script the ending.

Leaving the office, he took the back staircase down to the Studio level. Flashing red lights indicated taping was in progress. When they stopped, he opened the double Studio doors and tiptoed onto the Floor. No one stopped him. Those who did casually glance at him neither reacted nor challenged him. Stage hands and Prop men were making adjustments to the Bank set that was to be shot next. Three of the five cameras headed toward the set propelled by their cameramen. Clovis sidled behind the scenery to make his way down to the far end of the Studio where the one permanent standing set, the Sheraton Library with its magnificent unmoveable curved stairway, was positioned. Dark cul-de-sac.

Only the basic pieces of furniture were on the set—piano, piano bench, arm chairs, sideboard, sofa and coffee table. All hand props and lamps had been removed.

The set was angled in such a way that unless the cameras approached it directly, it was very difficult to see any action. It would have been very possible for Wally and his killer to have a sotto-voce confrontation without anyone in the studio being aware. Especially, if they were seated on the sofa. Clovis sat on it to watch the Bank set in motion. Joey Savage, the Stage Manager, held a small chalk-marked slate in front of camera #3 manned by Lester Williams. Joey read script number, date and scene from the slate and quickly ducked behind the camera, reciting "Five, four, three . . . . . ."

Maxwell Arden, playing Dwight Edgerton, walked into the set, patted his pompadour and addressed young Antonio Brunetti, playing Bart Lansing. "Young man, in my day young people had respect for money. What makes you think you can have access to a sum like this while you are still wet behind the ears." Bart answered, "Yoiks! Now you're going to tell me how you walked five miles through the snow to get to school."

"Hold it." Chuck's voice could be heard over the Public Address System as the actors stopped and looked up. "Max, I'm told you could be seen reading the teleprompter. Sorry."

"Places. Okay, Take Two," said Joey throwing the rechalked slate in front of the camera again.

Standing up, Clovis reached under the sofa cusions. Pages upon pages of script with character names and speeches marked by see-through yellow magic marker. "Lily." That would be Maggie List. "Samantha." Tracy George. Didn't they ever clean the place? Raising the cushion, he sifted through various discarded scenes. "From Day One," Maggie had said. Schedules covered with doodles. A neatly typed list of script notes embroidered by a green pentel. He recognized Wally's intricate handwriting, circled about various initials. Folding it carefully, Clovis placed it in his left shirt pocket.

Leaving the cushion up in hopes that some stage hand would take pity on the furniture, he skirted behind the scenery and, hearing Max fumble, he left the Studio.

Two hours later, boot soles against the oval table, posterior deep in swivel chair, Clovis watched the large televison screen through the spread knees of his Levis. The answer to both murders lay in that damned box.

On screen, Yancey as Sally Deering Brown Cartwright took measured steps toward the large desk in Lawyer Gray Lansing's empty office. Dressed rather sedately for Sally in a too tight brown wool suit, beige blouse with huge bow at the throat and small brown feather pillbox hat on the back of her upswept hair. She sat on the edge of the desk and looked away from camera. In profile, the slight hook in her nose, complimented by her strong jaw line gave her the look of a handsome filly. Slowly she turned toward the camera with a bemused smile as the camera moved in slowly for an extreme close-up and Sally's theme music gentled in. As her blue eyes, accentuated by beige eye-shadow, filled the screen, a slow dissolve went through to Sally with her hair down lying prone in pink satin sheets on a huge bed wearing the very skimpy nightgown. The fantasy had begun as the music segued to "I've Had The Time of My Life." In a rosy glow, the huge candelabras on either side of the bed sparkled as the candle flames burst in stars. As the camera closed in on Sally's cleavage, a hand came slowly into the shot and, taking Sally's hand, pulled her to her feet and to the naked breast of Jeff Landon who, as Gray Lansing, was wearing only pajama bottoms. She looked up at him adoringly. He put his arm around her and they began to slow, slow dance around the bed with dissolves from close-ups to long shots. Lingering on her eyes, his mouth, his eyes, her mouth.

Clovis watched Yancey as Sally. Head thrown back. Graceful. Erotic. How many women watching the scene wanted to be Yancey in Jeff's arms? How many men fantasized the feel of Yancey in their arms? Put themselves in Jeff's place and felt her soft breasts against their naked chests. Hundreds. If one were to believe the fan mail. Some yearning. Some sweet. And more than a few sickos. Fantasy. The backbone of Daytime world.

Clovis smiled to himself as he remembered his first sexual encounter with Yancey. Who had done the leading? He had just driven her to his rented apartment high above Ocean Avenue in Santa Monica. They'd gone out on the balcony for the picture postcard view of the ocean. He'd taken a cigarette, the Gauloise to which he was addicted, and lit it with his gold Zippo lighter.

Without looking at him, she'd said, "If you were free, I'd ask you to marry me."

"I'm free," he'd answered.

SHE:   Then consider this a proposal.

 HE:   I'll consider.

SHE:   One thing. You'll have to stop smoking.

 HE:   I may if you mean it.

SHE:   You don't trust me.

 HE:   I don't know you well enough yet.

SHE:   (taking cigarette out of his mouth) Why do you smoke?

 HE:   To put something in my mouth. I have nothing else to put in my mouth.

SHE:   I can take care of that. (Or was it, "I can do better than that"?)

 HE:   May I seduce you back inside?

SHE:   You already have.

He had taken her hand and they walked slowly together through the balcony door into the living room. She'd suddenly broken away and removed an elaborate gold Elsa Peretti barrette from her hair and tossed it carelessly on the glass top table. "Let's lose that," she'd said, "before one of us gets hurt."

On the screen, Sally had fallen back on the bed and just as Gray was moving to top her, a voice said "Sally!" and there was an abrupt cut back to Sally in Gray's office as the music stopped. Then Gray in pinstriped business suit entered the frame and said angrily, "What are you doing here?" A cut back to Sally, three tones of suspense chords and a fade to black. Commercials would be cut in and the question would be answered the next day. Stay tuned.

The phone jangled. "Kelley here."

"Darling, they just have to check the tape to make sure it's okay and then I can get out of this drag. Do you have anything you must do tonight or do I have you?"

"You've got me."

"Great," said Yancey. "What do you want to do first?"

"Fuck!"

"I wondered who was using this office," said Michael Ryan, the night Studio Manager, as he opened the door to the Producer's Office. "I saw Kelley leaving with Yancey a while back so I knew it wasn't him."

Vickie Jessup peered at him over her tortoise-shell Ben Franklin's. "Only me." Papers were spread out over the oval table.

"Back to your old bad habits?" yawned Michael.

"Depends on what you're referring to," said Vickie, raising her eyebrows.

"Working all these dumb hours," he explained, stroking his unshaven chin.

"I've got to get caught up for tomorrow's story meeting. By the way, I had dinner with your mother the other night. Looking good."

"She's okay for a rich lady," he grinned. "Buy you a cup of coffee later?"

"Truthfully, I'm kind of beat. As soon as I get through these outlines, I'm heading straight for the sack. Rain check?"

"You're on," he grinned. "And remember, it's only television. It ain't brain surgery."

Nice man. Maybe it would be a smart idea to offer him the now open Associate Producer's job. Political? Definitely. Gina didn't have the class or experience. Michael was very bright, a fast learner and had been brought up with the show. Allie wouldn't dare challenge that one. Good thinking, she complimented herself. Covering *all* bases!

The private line lit up a second before the ring and she grabbed the receiver. "Hello," Vickie said cautiously. "Thank God it's you. "I've been waiting here hoping you could get away." Her voice shifted into sexy. "I need you, baby. I'm aching. Okay. Of course I understand. Consider yourself kissed in all your wet places," she whispered, "love you." Sighing, she hung up the phone. Straight for the sack—alone.

Betsy Simpson sat crosslegged, back straight, thumbs and forefingers touching, eyes closed. "Ooom. Ooom. Ooom," she intoned. Gypsy, lying on the floor close to her crossed ankles, opened one eye and closed it again. She'd been there before. And before. Betsy raised her head and opened her eyes. Somewhere in a blaze of milky white light, a shrouded Wally smiled down on them.

*The murderer sat in the dark glaring back at the malevolent eye of the television set. Neutral. Equal. They were all equal. Big Brother joined all who watched into a fellowship that shared its glowing secret. The secret was in the box and the box was empty! Echoes of laughter played and replayed.*

# Chapter 9

Allie Jones stood at the window of her corner office on the 21st floor of the United Broadcasting System's Building. She pushed her pale-rimmed eyeglasses further up over the bridge of her nose to see the changing traffic patterns on Sixth Avenue more clearly. Buses. Yellow taxis. Cars. Vans. Snaking suicidal bicycles. People. Symbols on a distant computer game. Zap. Zap. Could this be the basis of a Game Show? "Patterns?" "Traffic?" No. A Monopoly style board game but no WHEEL OF FORTUNE or JEOPARDY. Some new approach to shore up the sagging UBS Daytime schedule. What?

She slowly took a hairpin out of the mass of swirled hair she liked to think of as her "Kate Hepburn do," and gathering other strands of her light brown hair, reconnected the pin at a more distant corner of the bird's nest. That's the audience down there. Each dot a potential viewer. Why the hell weren't they home, glued to their TV screens instead of jaywalking. She wanted to believe they all had VCRs set to capture the morning UBS line-up.

Raising her head she looked North. Central Park lay sprawled in front of her. To the left she could see the arch of the George Washington Bridge. To the right, past the white on blue waving Plaza flag, beyond Fifth Avenue lay the intricate hump of a nameless Railroad trestle. The Metropolitan Museum looked like a silver paperweight. The lakes and trees made her nostalgically homesick for the simpler years when she had simpler desires, goals. When she and the late J.T. Jones were first married in

Honesdale, Pennsylvania and dreamed of going to New York and raising a family. And those first years living in Brooklyn when she was a secretary and the biggest challenge was to get home in time to shop for and prepare the loin of pork so it would be ready for J.T.'s arrival from work. She straightened her shoulders and lowered her head slowly, feeling the notches in her neck pop.

Wally's death had not turned out to be the boon to ratings that she hoped it might be. Patrick had quickly put the lid on any exploitation. It would be great copy in a few years in *The Enquirer.* Long after it would be of help to her. And then poor, silly self-important Nora. Somehow murder belonged more in fiction than fact. The intellectual exercise was fun. The emotional reality was sordid. If Mr. Kelley ever found the murderer, it would make a great story line for KEY. Or had it been done already? A lot of story could get used up in fifteen years.

Buzz. She checked her Tiffany desk clock. "Yes, send him in." Right on time was Mr. Kelley. Unconsciously, she fluffed the sides of her hair and checked its silhouette against the reflection of the Hockney Irises. "Clovis! Thank you so much for coming to see me here. There are too many ears at the Studio." As she shook hands with him, she held his right hand in both of hers, tilted her head to the right and looked up at him. He was almost too handsome. Maybe he had a lousy body? Not the way his shoulders rippled under his loose grey linen jacket. Why would a man like this be interested in a twit like Yancey! "Please sit down," she said leading him to the overstuffed sofa with The View.

As she indicated Manhattan North, Clovis felt that she presented it with the same gesture Vanna White made when showing a category. Too bad she wasn't as adorable. She hadn't brought him all the way here to show off New York. Obligatory acknowledgement: "New York at its best."

"A magnificent kaleidescope." Good word. Was there a show in "kaleidescope" as a concept? She shifted her gaze from the window to Clovis. He crossed his legs and waited. He was waiting for her to start. Her hands flew to her hair. "I realize it's only been a few days since Wally's—demise and it is a very, very large canvas but Management," she moved her eyes ceiling-ward indicating the upper echelons on the higher floors, "has asked me for a progress report. They seem to feel one can issue a progress report as easily as a monthly status report." A slight smile and nervous gestures with fingers. "I'm on the carpet once a month."

He tried to contain it, but he couldn't. He broke into a deep laugh. "Sorry, somehow the visual of you on the carpet being prodded by men in business suits—" He guffawed.

She tittered. "It's really nothing like that. I report on each show's financial and rating status. And make them aware of impending problems such as one of the more popular actors not wanting to renew a contract because of the Call of the Coast. Primetime."

"It's quite a tall order to keep all the shows in perspective and also, I imagine, work on new projects." Perhaps it was a compliment that would erase his gaffe.

"Yes, it is. Each show has a liason person at the network who reports to me. But then, too, I'm on a very friendly, personal basis with the producers. Let's face it, I hired them."

"Then you were responsible for Wally being on the show?"

"Well, yes. Tillie was quite unhappy with Vickie. Thought she was burned out. I looked for a replacement and Wally came very highly recommended. He was on the Coast and wanted to come back to New York. I think there was some trouble that he wanted to distance himself from. A woman, no doubt." She smiled ruefully. "It's such a shame when a man lets his sexual appetite take precedence over his other talents."

"Do you remember who brought Wally to your attention?" Clovis asked.

"Is that important?" she asked with a slight tinge of irritability.

"It might be helpful."

Allie stood up to remove her outer layer, a baggy, knee-length red tweed jacket that matched her mid-calf skirt. A loose-knit yellow cotton sweater covered a navy T shirt. "It might have been his agent. I think he was with Morris. Or was it DMC? Damon Mandel's Company. Or it may have been my lawyer. Wally wanted to come East and on one of my monthly trips to California—we do most of our game shows out there—we met." She stopped abruptly and, pushing her glasses back over the bridge of her nose, faced Clovis. She stared at him for a moment and he stared back at her.

Well, Ms. Jones, thought Clovis, are you going to tell me the whole story or do I have to drag it out of you. "A charming man," Clovis prompted. "You were with him at David Bigelow's party as I remember."

"Yes," she said after a moment. "Charming. And destructive." Deep breath. "I do believe Wally was his own worst enemy." Right hand stroking neck. Change of approach. "Well, do you have anything 'to report'?"

The school-marmish tone made him flash on the small lonely boy in Ridgefield Grammar School. By the age of ten he'd learned how to cope. Don't answer. Question. "Why would anyone think that Wally's death would solve anything?"

"I'm sure I don't know," she answered defensively.

"Especially since he was about to be fired," said Clovis factually.

"Who told you that?" She looked startled.

"Tillie Ryan. She said that only you and she and Patrick were aware of that." He watched her accept the news with relief. "As much as he ruled the show with a bully's smugness, the most he could really do was get someone to lose their job. And, in the world of television, from what I gather, it's Peter Principle. The very fact that you hired him proved that. Who had something important, truly earth shattering so that Wally had to be silenced?"

"Tillie Ryan," she answered quickly. "She has the biggest stake. If the show fails, she loses millions. And prestige."

"And you?" asked Clovis quietly.

"Me?" Allie flushed. Never let them see you sweat. "THE KEY TO LIFE is not the only show on the Daytime line-up. Any examination of any of the ratings services—not just Nielsen— proves that UBS is way ahead of the other networks in Daytime. Primetime should look so good!" she added aggressively.

"On the day Wally was killed you were at the Studio. Do you go there often?"

"Occasionally. KEY has the best support personnel. Hair. Make-up. So I go there to get made over when I have to do something special. Network parties. Shareholders meetings. Affiliates. I was there *that* day on a long story meeting. Frankly, I prefer them away from the Studio but Wally felt he had to be there. And, he would never sacrifice a weekend to work."

"Who is in these meetings? Always the same people?" asked Clovis.

"Outline meetings take place every week with Tillie and Dewey, her Head Writer, Nora, Marti, my assistant, and the Producer. I'm the one addition when long story meetings take place about every four or six months depending on what problems arise. We try to play story lines to cover long periods of time. You see, all soaps start out with a bible, which is literally that. It blocks out the characters, theme, story lines in general that will develop over the years. Of course, as the characters are cast and one sees audience reactions, alterations take place."

He watched her start to relax as she explored familiar territory. "Tillie is the one who wrote the bible?"

"Eighteen years ago, she conceived KEY and took it to Patrick. She had known him when he was Head of Sales and she had been Head Writer on THE HOUSE OF HADLEY. She had a good track record and the approach was fresh with an upbeat theme. 'Love is the key to life.' It was a natural and Patrick turned it over to me. Tillie and I worked together to get the show on the air." Said with pride.

"That's a long marriage," Clovis commented.

"We've had our disagreements but I think we respect each other. I must admit that Tillie is a genius in dreaming up characters. You start with your tent pole character who holds the soap in place and branch out from there. After the actors are cast, their voices, intonations and personalities take over so the writers write for the actor as well as the role. As for the story lines, as they unfold and other actors are added, they add branches to other story lines. Tillie will be the first to tell you that there are only about seven basic themes. Classic ones. Triangle," she started counting on her fingers, "fish out of water, odd couple, Romeo and Juliet, mistaken identity, Ugly Duckling, Othello. Variations of these, depending on characters and mores, make for a wide variety of plots."

"Fascinating. And all this comes from Tillie's obviously very fertile brain."

"With a little help from her friends," Allie preened.

"So you are all locked up in the creative process and take breaks at the same time?"

"More or less. We break about every hour. Pee break! And so Wally could smoke a borrowed cigarette. Send out for lunch. Most meetings can't last longer than five hours. Brain fag sets in."

"Does everyone contribute during these long story meetings?" Clovis asked.

"Usually Tillie has notes that we discuss and change. Yes, we all have something to say. Marti and Nora basically took notes. The Producer usually has suggestions. And, after we have a general agreement on the shape of stories to come, Tillie goes home and dictates a document to her secretary that gets distributed to us for minor changes. Then the breakdown writers take over and the outlines emerge that are discussed in the weekly meetings. I read the outlines and give my notes to Marti."

"Certainly is a complicated process. Where does Dewey Dakin

fit into all this. I've been led to believe that creativity is not his long suit," Clovis smiled.

"I won't ask where you heard that. Dewey is most necessary to Tillie. He is brilliant in keeping the show within its clerical and financial boundaries. Contractual guarantees. Number of sets. Assignments of the outlines to the dialoguers who actually write the scripts. He keeps all the relationships straight and does the checking with medical sources and other research necessities."

"That's quite a job. It must be difficult to have a precision oriented job in a creative environment," said Clovis with admiration.

"It is frustrating for him since he can correct problems but cannot deal with them in an inventive way. But he's healthy about it. He works out at the gym at least four times a week."

"The Y?"

"The Y?" Allie covered her mouth with her hand. "The Y! Dewey wouldn't set foot in a place like that. No. The New York Athletic Club protects him from having to play handball with someone who is not socially acceptable."

Metallic knock. The door opened slightly to allow one of Marti Liverski's heavily padded shoulders into the office. "Oh, sorry," she whined, smiling. "I didn't know you had anyone with you." Like hell she didn't, thought Allie. Marti waved a sheaf of papers. "Focus session results." Then, as if noticing Clovis for the first time, turned to him and said, "Oh! Hi." Putting her hands behind her back, she rested them on Allie's desk and arched her back emphasizing the full heft of her breasts.

Allie's annoyance took the form of heavy lip pursing. Rabbit twitches. "Clovis was giving me a report."

Clovis stood up. "Thanks for seeing me," he smiled his whitest at Allie. "I'll be in touch."

As he left the office, Marti turned to Allie and whispered, "What did he say? What does he know?"

Allie straightened her back and assumed her best executive pose. "I'm sorry, Marti. I'm not in a position to repeat what he said. It's privileged information." She was pleased by Marti's startled look. Just as well Marti believed that Clovis had told *her* something confidential. Never would she admit, even to Patrick, he hadn't told her one damn thing.

Years ago, David Bigelow would have reacted to Clovis Kelley's study with an amazed "Wow!." Now he acknowledged it with a simple, "nice." It was a large ultra-modern gallery lit white-washed brick room in the East 62nd Street brownstone Clovis had inherited from his mother's bachelor lawyer brother. A row of midnight-blue file cabinets lined one wall. Over them hung a full-breasted antique Lorelie masthead and a huge weathered green copper lion's head. An enormous two-way window looked out on a miniature English garden. At the ceiling was a ribbon of steel from which a motion picture screen could be lowered.

"Segal?" asked David of the white plaster figure of Clovis seated in a Bentwood rocker tugging at his right sideburn.

"Yes," said Clovis, gathering papers from the nine foot glass-topped tempered steel table he used as a desk. He took the papers to the parquet table in front of the long red, yellow and navy paid couch and sat next to David.

"When I told you I had stories about Wally," said David, "I was not aware that one of them was going to do him in. No, I don't know which one and chances are you have more stories than I."

"Very possibly," Clovis admitted. "That's why I have a lot of questions for you."

"Ask away," said David. "However, there's something I have to know." He paused and played with the gold earring dangling from his right earlobe. "Truthfully, didn't you ever want to be an actor?"

"Et tu, Dave." Clovis shook his head negatively.

"Okay. Okay." David grinned, raising his hands in an arrest

mode. "All I know is that if I had looked like you, I'd still be acting. It's a hell of a lot easier and more lucrative than writing."

"Why'd you quit acting?" asked Clovis.

"I was too lightweight. I didn't have your teeth, voice or stature. In short, I wasn't leading man material. Also, maybe down deep I knew I wasn't good enough to cut it."

"That takes guts."

"I've got a few," David smiled and stroked his beard. "You can take the boy out of the actor but you can't take the actor out of the man. Maybe. Maybe when I'm old enough to be a wizened character man, I'll drift on back. But for now I love being Head Writer of THE HOUSE OF HADLEY. Writing a soap is exciting. You can stretch your imagination. Explore your own head and have a wonderful time. Soaps are built on the two great pillars of Secrets and Fantasy. You can weave and interweave. Flash forward. Flash back. Name it. Night soaps have the bucks to show off but they haven't the time for depth. It's fast and dirty on tape. Love it!"

"Living up at the Studio the last few days has been a revelation. It's a miracle to me that a complete hour show gets churned out every day with as much quality as it has. Every day a small toy village comes to life. Amazing! How do you rate Vickie Jessup as a Producer?" Clovis asked.

"Well, she's a slight bit anal. She can put chaos in order and make everyone enjoy themselves. But, she's so uptight that it gets in the way sometimes."

"Why?" asked Clovis.

"Can we come back to that?" David asked. He got up from the couch and stretched.

"All right," said Clovis, puzzled. "You're the only person I know who is familiar with those involved with KEY, and, at the same time, is distanced from it. You started out as a writer on KEY, didn't you?"

"Yes," said David, sitting down again. "As you are aware, many actors become writers. When I faced my waning acting career, I wrote a sample script based on KEY characters and sent it to Tillie Ryan. I had met her with Yancey. Tillie was great. She called me in and explained what I had done right and what I had done wrong and told me to keep watching the show. Then when one of the staff dialoguers quit, Tillie gave me a crack at it. I worked for Tillie—she owned the writing package before she sold the show to the Network—for several years, hopefully working my way up to be an outline writer. I had ideas popping off the top of my head. Tillie was very receptive. Dewey was not. He found me too aggressive. Tillie helped me get a job on HADLEY as an outline writer. And here I am as Head Honcho on HOUSE OF HADLEY —a quadruple "H" man."

"And worth every penny," smiled Clovis. "Here, look at this," he handed David a list. "The KEY lineup:

       32 Production Staff
       28 Technical
       59 Engineers
        9 Security and Air Conditioning
       22 Assorted—

Assorted means Make-up, Hair, Studio Managers, Unit Managers, Teleprompter. That comes to One Hundred and Fifty people without counting the Actors, Writers or Network executives. And they were all underfoot on that day. On the day Wally was murdered there was a total cast of 53 which includes contract players, day players and extras and under fives."

"A mere bagatelle," David smiled. "If they'd been doing a courtroom scene or a party, the actors could have come to over one hundred. And, you've managed to boil this mass down?"

"I have about fifteen to twenty contenders. Each of them was there and also had a motive. I think. That's where I can use your input."

"Have you run the list past Yancey?" asked David.

"In some respects but not specifically. She's too close and too emotionally involved with some of them. It's not easy to believe that a close friend can commit murder—no matter how warranted," said Clovis.

"I must tell you I am not completely impartial," David paused. "There are two people involved with KEY whom I love very much. Yancey, as you know, is one of them. As for the other, when I said I was seeing you today, I asked permission to tell you the truth about our relationship."

"I assume it's the best kept secret in the business," Clovis said smiling.

David did not return the smile. "Yes, it is. Though we have been involved for well over a year, we didn't want anyone to know until we ourselves knew the depth of our involvement. Then Wally came on the scene and he would have made mince-meat of us. We're a very odd combination and we love each other very much. Whatever our needs, we've been happily satisfying them. We've been wanting to come out of the closet. I've been longing for Yancey to know. We both have."

Clovis was grateful for the training which kept his face sans expression. He studied David as the writer stroked his beard thoughtfully. Slender, boyish, trendy dresser. Tick-weave silk vest, ramie-linen and cotton trousers, cotton striped and dotted shirt. Ensemble courtesy of Ralph Lauren. Foulard blue and rose tie. He obviously liked spending his money and knew how to create a visual. The ex-actor was now writing a scene for himself.

"I hope the person isn't one of my suspects. Not that suspect means murderer. I still feel in my gut that whoever did in Wally was also responsible for Nora's death. A sudden impulse triggered by one of Wally's better putdowns caused his death. Nora was a case of wrong place, wrong time busy-body." Clovis nattered on, giving David time to pull himself together so he could name his lover.

David stood up and pressed his hands against his vest. He walked to the two-way window and looked out at the garden.

Finally, he turned to Clovis. "It's Maud. Maud Sterling. She has children older than I."

"She's not one of my suspects," commented Clovis.

"She should be," said David evenly. "But I think she should tell you about it herself."

Yancey walked slowly up the hilly block between Amsterdam and Columbus Avenues. 81st Street. In her right hand was the heavy plastic white, blue skyed with black skyscrapers shopping bag from Fairway crammed with arugula, basil, bib lettuce, firm broccoli, avocado and cherry tomatoes. In her left hand she carried the white roped handles of the orange lettered Zabar's bag. It was stuffed with easily half the goodies listed on either face of the bag. Nodding to the old black man who sat with his tattered hound on the same stoop each day, she enjoyed being a real New Yorker. A true Yupper West Sider. She loved the feel of a small town neighborhood. Not quite like Lubbock but she still had the warm glow of knowing the Korean in the liquor store, the yamalked tailor at the dry Cleaners, the Hispanic lady at the Drug store, the Israeli at the kiosk. Also, it was a very easy walk to the Studio. No taxi worries.

Yancey loved to cook when she was not working. Tonight she was making dinner for three of her favorite people. Clovis, David Bigelow and Maud. David had called her after confessing to Clovis and she had called Maud and, after a good cry for both over the telephone, it was agreed they would all celebrate tonight together. She loved both David and Maud, and if it pleased him to ball a woman old enough to be his mother, that was A-Okay with her. Chacun à son goût. It certainly explained why he had grown a beard, which aged him. She only hoped that they were as happy as she was with Clovis. Her eyes welled and she started to hum "Sentimental Old Me."

As she reached the end of the block, she put the bags down to get the keys out of her blue canvas tote that also contained the filets from the Nevada market. She became aware that footsteps that she had heard behind her from the time she rounded the corner at the Cosy Chinese Restaurant, had stopped abruptly. Turning slowly, she thought she saw someone drop down the stairs of the Travel Bureau. So what? Just an eerie feeling. Imagination working overtime and there wasn't time for that now.

Yancey lived in a small Co-op building which had been converted from three tenements into sixteen lofts. She had fallen in love with the fireplaces, high ceilings and sunlit views of the Museum of Natural History Park. She could also make-believe that 81st Street toward the Park was a Parisian Boulevard. It was so wide. Buying two adjoining lofts, one of which was a duplex, she had built an apartment to her specific needs. A very large kitchen-dining area and only one bedroom. Exposed brick and wood panelling gave her a home that she liked to think of as a Connecticut house in the middle of Manhattan. She often teased Clovis that, as a former Connecticut native, he had fallen in love with her apartment rather than her. She found his house a bit too formal for her tastes.

After depositing the bags in the kitchen, she checked the answering machine. The digital read-out of the Code-A-Phone read zero. That was odd. Barbie was always very prompt about telling her when her call for the next day would be and giving her whatever cuts and changes the director might have made in the script. The clock radio beside the bed read 4:39. She pressed the "message" bar on the machine. Barbie's piping voice said, "Your call tomorrow is 8:30 which should make you happy. And you haven't any cuts or changes. See you." Dial tone. "Hi, babe," said Clovis' voice, "I'll be there 6:30ish. Since I understand they'll be there 7:00, don't get any funny ideas. Ciao. Oh yes, afterthought, I love you." Then the machine went dead-sounding, which meant no further messages. Yancey pressed the rewind bar. Strange. Was the machine broken? Had Clovis' reluctant admission put it on the fritz? Stupid! Was there some connection with this machine upset and all those hang-up calls? Was someone trying to spook her? 4:45. No time to feel creepy or worry it out now. Set the table first and then clean the veggies and the salad. She'd never be ready.

Turning the Water Pik Shower Massage to its fifth extreme, Clovis felt the pounding release the knots in his shoulders. Cut yourself some slack, boy, and relax, he told himself. There's no smart ass Trivial Pursuit answer. Just because David's insights were not enough to help you pinpoint the murderer doesn't mean that you've lost your touch. You're a long way from belly up on this case. Hell, it ain't even a week.

Soaping himself with Guerlain Geranium Sapocetti (Yancey said the odor lingered deliciously), he started to review his list of suspects. Motive and opportunity. Not once but twice. With David's knowledge of some of the people involved, he had dismissed a few borderline suspects. Though Maggie List and Tracy George were high on the roster of those whose jobs were threatened by Wally, neither of them were psychologically or physically capable of that murder—no matter how much adrenaline had been pumped.

Closer to home was Johnny Krog, number three son. Had the constant humiliation by his father finally driven Johnny to kill him: Patricide was usually much bloodier. Pent up anger used an ax, not a knitting needle. And during Nora's fall, he'd been with his mother. Double check that alibi? Yes. But doubtful.

Crew? Only three had motives and opportunity for both murders. Large, ambling Moe Chernin for one. A lot of suppressed passion in that shuffling old man. Made it clear he didn't like either of them. And, he had found Nora's body. Possible suspect.

As were both Frank Quinn and Lester Williams. Frank, the gentle giant Shop Steward on Camera #2. One of Wally's best playmates. But, disillusioned by false promises, could he have turned? The back staircase was used almost exclusively by the crew so he could have encountered Nora with a karate chop leaned during his sessions with Wally at the Y. As could Lester Williams, Camera #3. A lover's quarrel? Motive for killing Wally could have been that he never got over having his sexual preferences decorating the men's room in green ink. Both cameramen were definitely still suspects.

Chuck Rosen, the director. Larger than life and bravado on all fronts. David had insights into Chuck's possible motive. A gambler, Chuck was always in debt. He could not afford to be out of work for one second. Unless that second was on a helicopter to Atlantic City. High Roller! He would have to have been very fleet footed to sprint down the length of the Studio without anyone noting. And Nora? No. Very doubtful.

Bud Easton, Nora's husband, could not be ruled out. Jealous of Wally's influence on her? Could also be he found out there was fire beyond the smoke of the Nora-Lester relationship. The records had shown that a call had been made from Nora's private office line to the Easton home in New Jersey at the time Bud had stated. An answering machine could have picked up. Bud was a possible suspect despite the timing of Wally's murder. He was a familiar figure around the Studio. Check next to Bud Easton.

In the Support group there were really only two people who had specific motives re Wally. Re Nora, it was just that she needled them constantly about getting in on time. Jolie Dornya, jilted lover, was an obvious choice. Her temper, passion and erratic personality keyed her in place as a potential killer. But, chances were that Jolie featuring herself as Jeanne d'Arc, would have dramatically admitted what she'd done and thrown herself on the mercy of the court—a crime passionelle.

Mark Golden's motive could only be to avenge the wrong done his lover, Arthur. That was hardly in character. As David pointed out, there was no end to the misinformation disseminated by those two hairburners!

Production. Leading all suspects was Victoria Jessup. The conveniently in the wrong place at the right time "Mayor." She needed the job for her ego, her identity. But there was no proof that she would have gotten it. Had a deal been cut someplace? Was murder part of it? She was athletic and, seemingly in good shape. David refused to discuss his earlier evasiveness but that seemed based on a long standing friendship. He didn't feel Vickie was capable. Well, someone had to be. Vickie was still high on his list of suspects.

Gina Serpente. Humiliation was a very poor motive. And, though she was paper-thin fragile, maybe her unseen friend, Mr. Pasquale Giambroni, wanted to defend her honor. Corny? Bullshit. Losing your marbles, Clovis asked himself as he stepped out of the shower and started to towel dry himself.

And the network duo. Alice Jones and her assistant Marti Livorski. If he interpreted Wally's datebook right, they both had fucked him. Allie knew he was going to be fired and he threatened her? Patrick would not like that information. Wally was very dangerous for Mrs. Alice Jones. As David said, he'd seen her turn from sparrow to vulture in seconds. She was in the right place for Wally's murder. It was also possible she'd gone to the Studio for the Hair and Make-up treatment so she'd look her best for her appearance at the funeral parlor the night of Nora's death. Moving up on the list.

As for Marti, what if the husband found out? Was Wally worth the marriage? Marti was a woman who had to have a husband backing her up. She needed Lincoln Livorski to parade at the right times and *she* would decide when they were. And, she loathed Nora. Possible?

And let us not forget Matilda Listman Ryan. But why would Tillie kill him if she could get him fired? Blackmail? A passionate and earthy woman. But not a stupid one. Too clever for murder. Or was she? David was positive Tillie could not have done it. But could she have inspired someone else? Who? Her son? Dewey? Not very likely.

Actors. Jeff R. Landon. Fear of exposure. (No pun intended.) Had Wally been blackballing him. (No pun intended.) Jeff had the intensity, strength and opportunity. As for Nora, she was too inquisitive. Jeff was a possible suspect.

Maxwell Arden. As much as he hated Wally and feared his reputation was at stake, he was not a passionate man. Nora was aware he was stacking the fan mail. And that was why Nora altered Barbie's fan mail list numbers. She always lowered the number of letters Max received to a reasonable amount so the Network could put him in perspective and not star him in his own series. Some motive to kill her. Old fool would be more likely to talk them to death.

And now there was Maud. He was most interested in what motive she might have. She did have the opportunity but somehow her character profile didn't skew. Was she just wanting to keep stage center?

Clovis counted. From the original list of over two hundred people who were available to have murdered Wally, he had reduced the list to eight. Eight to murder Wally, eight to kill Nora. Moe Chernin, Frank Quinn, Lester William, Bud Easton, Vickie Jessup, Allie Jones, Marti Livorski and last but not least, Jeff R. Landon. He ran mental film clips trying to envision each of them jabbing a knitting needle into Wally's thick neck with a lucky hit on the aorta. Or giving Nora an expert Karate chop. He couldn't get any of them to really materialize.

Damn! Why was the zoo still closed. It was such a comfort to walk through the park and commune with the beasts. Only truly pleasant, attractive beings in this world. Straightening his silver on gold links Hermes tie, he looked at himself in the mirror. Echoes of Michael Jackson. Yes, the man in the mirror *is* me. Slightly altered but that was another life with another woman.

I'll get the answer to this puzzle, he told himself. It lies somewhere within THE KEY TO LIFE itself.

Maud Sterling was always "on." The energy of a kitten, the grace of a panther, she admitted to sixty-two. Those who measured in tabloid years, came closer to sixty-eight. "You can't tell me she was nine years old when she played Dion Mackintosh's wife in THE GLORIOUS JADES. I'll believe sixteen, even fifteen, but nine? NEVER!" Ignoring any logic, Maud's response was always a delighted admission. "Face lifts. Darling, I've had two. There's no way I could look this young without the help of that wonderful Dr. Ju. David Ju is the best plastic surgeon in the city. Plus, of course, exercise and a very strict diet regime. As I get older, I am more and more in tune with that adage that says: to stay youthful one must have a good dentist and a young lover. And, praise be, I've got both."

Proud of the subtle uplift of her molded breasts (Dr. Ju, too?) and her long, shapely legs, in public Maud always wore haut, haut couture creations with low cleavage and slit skirts. The give-away brown speckled hands were either pancaked or gloved. Though the hundreds of yearly interviews varied (she was notorious for speaking to anyone who printed), they all included that she'd been in the business since she was discovered at a Spelling Bee in Evanston, Illinois by that lecherous old man, the infamous and talented Dion Mackintosh. Not wanting a cradle-snatching stigma, Dion claimed Maud to be older than she was. "And you know how teenagers always want to be older, more mature. The Big Screen in its Silver Days was a wonderful testament to one's youth. But, it's no fun to watch yourself age in living color. The small screen's imprecisions are much kinder to older stars." She still considered herself a leading lady and not a character actress.

A one-person lexicon of Entertainment Tonight, Maud had known or worked with almost everyone in *Who's What in Film*. "I plan to work until I drop. Dead that is! I plan to live even longer than Estelle. Winwood, who else? I don't waste my time mourning for the world that's gone. I look ahead. To the next century! Imagine, I have lived to learn that a way has been found to sterilize cockroaches before a cure for the common cold. Priorities. The problem with society today is that the crumbs making the uppercrust are only held together by dough. Well, I might have been a headache, but I never was a bore."

"A truer word was never spoken, my love," said David as they all moved from the dining area of Yancey's apartment into the living room. Clovis and Yancey settled into the rose paisley love seat between the windows. Standing in front of the fireplace, Maud smiled at David and raised her glass of brandy in a toast. "I have known many, liked not a few. Loved only one. I drink to you." She and David lightly touched glasses and then lips. Yancey beamed like a proud parent and nestled closer to Clovis.

Taking Maud's arm, David steered her to the pale blue sofa across from them. "Darling, the time has come for you to tell Clovis why you had a very real motive for killing Wally Krog."

Maud carefully placed her brandy snifter in the blue Wedgewood plate on the lacquered coffee table. She closed her eyes for a moment as a shudder ran through her body. She pressed her thumb and forefinger under her brow. Then shaking her head, she opened her eyes and, looking directly at Clovis, began to speak in low tones. "I've had three children. One with that lewd old man who seduced a virginal me. In those days, children were *not* 'born out of wedlock.' So the old fool divorced his patient wife of forty years and married me so that Dion, Junior could have a last name. He then divorced me and remarried the stolid Helga. At that time women who didn't paint or write or act forgave geniuses their transgressions. The glorious days when a Chevrolet was just that and not ten odd varieties with fancy names. Dion, Jr. had the bad taste to take after his father in everything but talent. He's ended up as the kept husband of some Hungarian Countess with whom he writes articles on food. I think they now live somewhere in what was once called Estonia.

"My second husband, Daniel Arrow, was part Indian and totally dashing, debonaire, debauched, divorced and drunk. He was a director. Daniel, Junior was a marvelous bright, happy boy who had the good sense to become a doctor, marry a rich Texas girl and have my three grandchildren. He is a highly successful surgeon in Ft. Worth." Maud paused and took a sip of the brandy. She turned toward David who put his arm around her shoulder. She leaned her head against his chest.

"Tell them, darling," he urged.

"And then there was my beautiful baby girl," Maud said, in almost a whisper. "Though I was still married to my decaying Daniel—who finally drank himself into the grave about twenty years ago—I had my first true love. Before David. It matters not who he was. His name did not start with a "D". What matters is that we could not be married because we both were. But I did have the child of our love, my dearest baby, Dorothea. Thea. A charmed, bright, gentle, golden girl. A beautiful, fairy-tale child. Imaginative and sensitive, she loved the world of make-believe. She loved to play-act and dreamt of becoming a real actress. I could deny her nothing. I allowed her to start with small roles in school plays. And those that saw her invited her to start with tiny parts in films. I was oh-so-careful what she played and with whom. And, we would discuss and examine and interpret all that she did and wanted to do. She was twenty when Wally killed her." Maud swallowed hard and shook her head. She squeezed David's hand so hard that his knuckles whitened.

David folded Maud's head into his chest. Hugging her, he continued. "Maud was on a long location shoot when Wally Krog, as director of a little non-union flick, offered Thea a cameo role that would be just a few days work. Sounded ideal. Part of a spunky college girl. So Maud approved by telephone. What he didn't mention was that there was a stunt involved. Seemed simple enough. Just jump out of the way of a car bearing down on you. Too cheap to hire stunt people, Wally cajoled Thea into doing it. And so Dorothea Arrow became another statistic. A footnote. He was very sorry, was Wally, but he wasn't driving the car. It was an accident, these things happen. So what if his buddy driving the car may have been drinking. Two years and time off for good behaviour. And with a few friends in the right places, it was hushed up. No point in giving the business a bad name."

Clovis watched Yancey as the tears spattered from her eyes. He handed her his handkerchief. Yancey went to Maud, embraced her and then knelt at her feet, putting her head in Maud's lap.

"Thank you," said Maud, dry eyed, stroking Yancey's hair. "I can't forgive or forget. That was eighteen years ago. For three years I was a zombie. A recluse. And then when they were desperately searching for familiar names, someone remembered I was alive. I was offered THE KEY TO LIFE. It *was* for me. I realized I had to go on with my life. And now God has given me the wondrous gift of David." They exchanged a long look. "Yes," Maud added, "I had the motive. I even prayed for the death of Wally and his buddy. I had the opportunity to kill him. But I didn't do it. I believe in looking forward, not backward."

Yancey got to her feet and blew her nose vigorously. "And you didn't even react when Wally was brought on to the show," she said with amazement.

"There wouldn't have been any point. It was a fait accompli. And revenge would only have made me as ugly as he was," Maud answered. "He was quite remarkable. When we were introduced, he tried to kiss my hand and tell me what a fan of mine he had always been. He was so happy to finally make my acquaintance!"

"Then you've been on KEY since it started," Clovis said to Maud. "Has it changed a great deal with the different producers?"

"You want my opinion?" Maud asked.

"Do you know what you're asking?" laughed David. "I'm going to get me another drink on that one. Any else?" They all raised their glasses. "I'll just bring the bottle."

"At my age I've got a right to be opinionated," Maud smiled at David's retreating figure. "The main trouble with KEY has always been the same. No Indians. All Chiefs. And like any unrelated group that works together over a long period of time, there are factions that form. Deadbeats who surface. But, eventually, like a true family, people become supportive of each other. That's why though some may hate each other all year long, comes Emmy time, and everyone bands together against the common enemy— anyone nominated from another show! Vickie used to call herself the Mayor. With good reason. I've always been very fond of Vickie and I'm thrilled she's back. She'll pull the people and the show together and we can have fun again. Wally pulled everyone apart. Why work someplace you hate going—yes, for the money!"

"Any favorites—besides Yancey?" asked Clovis.

"Jolie's amusing but not as good a hairdresser as Mark. I adore Jeff. I wish he'd sober up and grow up and he could be a really fine actor. Maggie is one of my favorite actors. Chuck Rosen would make a fine director if he'd trust his instincts instead of his formulas."

"What about the network, the crew, the writers? How do you feel about them?" asked Clovis as David circled with the bottle of Martell V.S.O.P.

"Frankly, I've never trusted one of them at the Network. Party line. Allie's always been afraid for her job. I always suspected that she fired Vickie because she heard somewhere that she was gay and thought it might reflect on her. Allie won't confront and will never take a stand. As for that Marti, she's like an animal who's always covering her tracks. But they're the same breed everywhere. Unqualified for anything but being an executive. As for the crew, they're basically a good group. Wally tried to be devisive but I'm not sure he succeeded because they all love the show and being part of it. As for the writers, I adore Tillie. Talented and wickedly vulgar. Dewey gives me a pain. I don't know how DeeDee has put up with him all these years."

"I don't think it's been that difficult," said Yancey. I've known DeeDee for years and years. And whenever she's on the show, she shares my dressing room and we have a lot of laughs."

"I didn't know you shared your dressing room," said Clovis.

"I really don't. But only the contract players have specific dressing rooms and when I'm not on, they may put a day player in there. The poor Extras have to hang out in the Rehearsal Hall until they're called because there's not enough room for them any place else. But since DeeDee and I are old pals, she always gets to use my dressing room whether I'm there or not." Yancey paused and looked at Clovis. "Yo! Yo, Clovis! Earth to Clovis. Where are you, darling," she asked, snapping her fingers in front of his face.

"Sorry. The gridlock in my brain was rearranging itself. I think you may have clued me into solving the murder," Clovis said.

"Me?" asked Yancey. David and Maud exchanged surprised looks.

"When I took the bus over here tonight—" Clovis started.

"Hold the phone," said David. "You took a bus?"

"The zoo was closed so I didn't feel like walking through the park. And when I don't walk, I often take the bus. I'm always fascinated to see that different bus lines carry totally divergent types. One of the interesting things is that M7 riders have nothing in common with the M104s."

Yancey turned to David. "What do you expect from someone who was named after his mother's dog. I told you he was mad."

"And your father named you after his favorite horse," David noted.

"Stop it, you two! I don't care what your animal farm connection might be," Maud interjected. "I want to know what happened on the bus that would help you know who the murderer could be."

"On the buses," Clovis explained, "for you who never ride them, they have cards with advertisements. Lately, there has been a series called 'Streetfare' that has poetry on the cards. There was one I saw this evening that I found myself memorizing. It was by someone called Carl Rakosi. I can't remember the title but it had something to do with rats. The poem went kind of like this:

'Whenever I nudge that spring a bell rings
And a man comes out of a cage assiduous and
    sharp like one of us
And gives me cheese.
How did he fall into my power.' "

"So?" asked Yancey.

"You know those optical tricks when you look at a box and it seems full. Then you shift your eyes and it seems empty. That's what I've been doing," said Clovis, growing excited. "I needed to tilt my thinking and I just have. I have a hunch who killed Wally. And Nora. Now all I have to do is prove it."

# Chapter 10

"Mmmmmm," Yancey murmured as she rolled over in her king sized bed and reached for Clovis. She felt the warm place where he had been, but her sleeping hand found no body. Yet he was there. She could smell the faint fragrance of the Guerlain. He was kissing her. A gentle cheek kiss. Was she dreaming? Slowly she opened her eyes. Clovis was bending over her.

"Go back to sleep," he smiled, "You still have a few hours."

"What time is it?" she asked, forcing her eyes open in an attempt to waken herself.

"Five."

"Five!" She tried to rub the sleep from her eyes and stared at him. "Five and you're shaved, showered and dressed?"

"Give the girl one hundred," he said, sitting on the edge of the bed.

"But you've had no sleep at all. We didn't turn out the lights to *sleep* until—"

"I am very aware what took place in this room last night after your guests left," said Clovis, savoring the memory.

"*Our* guests," Yancey teased as she raised her arms like a small child asking to be lifted.

Clovis stood up. "No, you don't. I have very little self control in the morning as you know too damn well. And you better get your beauty sleep or Make Up will run out of whitener and blush."

"Horrid man. Where are you going—"

"At this ungodly hour? To the Studio where I can have coffee and Danish with the crew. Ask a few questions that kept me awake. Then do my homework in Wally's office before the troops convene for their story meeting."

"Be careful. For me."

He kissed his index finger and placed it on her lips. "The things you've taught me," he said, shaking his head with disbelief.

"Only about loving. Loving 101. A minor course in human relationship that you seem to have skipped. I think you know most everything else."

"Would that I did," he said tucking the sheets around her. "I think the time may have come to buy you an expensive item from Tiffany. Or Cartier."

"What I want can't be bought at either store," Yancey said as she reached for him.

"I'll remember you said that," Clovis laughed, pulling away.

"Love you," she whispered and closed her eyes to try to snuggle back into her dream.

The Rehearsal Hall was in the throes of an exceptionally slow rehearsal despite the efforts of Chuck Rosen, the Director, to whip the actors awake.

A haggard Jeff Landon had swayed in ten minutes late, a styrofoam cup with black coffee in his shaking left hand. "Sorry," he mumbled, his blood shot eyes at half-mast.

"Thank you, your majesty, for coming into our presence," Chuck said between clenched teeth. "Into your set. Go." Chuck pointed to the mock set of Gray Lansing's office.

Jeff, head down, stumbled toward the set. "Sorry," he mumbled to an immaculate Max Arden who waited for him with a disdainful nose curling.

"Okay, from the top," said Chuck, "Jeff, you're at highboy. Go on. Move your bod. No, that is the desk," he pointed. "*That* is the highboy. It's your set and you should know it by now. Say your goddamned line about your dealings with the Police Department.

Blah, blah, blah and walk five steps toward the desk, count three and then turn around and deliver your next line."

"I tried to get the Police to drop the charges," Jeff read from the script in his right hand. He walked the five steps toward the desk and said, "they won't listen to me but—"

"Do you or do you not understand English," Chuck roared. "Did I not say count three and *then* turn around. I need time to cut to a shot of Max for his reaction."

Stop watches clicked and started again at the table where Trudy von Richter, the Associate Director, and Nickie Pastori, the Production Assistant, sat. "Here we go again," Trudy whispered to Nickie who was marking changes in the scripts for Music, Audio, Sound Effects and Teleprompter.

"What's the time?" asked Chuck.

"Two minutes, twenty-nine seconds," said Trudy.

"Figure the scene at two-fifteen. It will tighten if Mr. Landon can pull himself together and avoid the pauses. What's next?"

"Sally and Lily at the Hospital waiting room."

Chuck looked around the Rehearsal Hall. Lily, Maggie List, in her forever black, was sitting quietly on a sofa, knitting the teal blue sweater memorizing her lines. He marched to the wall phone that fed into the public address system. "Sally. Yancey. Yancey Howland. Where are you? We are waiting," he crooned.

"Look, I'm really sorry," Jeff said to him when he replaced the phone.

"And what did you do last night? Another video evening at home?"

"None of your business," Jeff growled.

Which Chuck knew meant yes. Another night at home with a bottle of Cutty Sark and an X-rated video. He'd heard that *Hard to Handle* was the most recent turnon. Poor lonely bastard, he thought. A bottle of Scotch and an X-rated video could satisfy all his lonely needs. If he was that drunk, how could he wack off? Maybe he didn't and that was the problem.

"Chuck, may I speak to you for a moment," asked Max as soon as Jeff walked away.

"Sure. Now we're waiting on Yancey. She's never late. Trudy, Nickie, check her dressing room, call her at home. *Do* something. Yes, Max, what is it?"

Max indicated with a tilt of his elaborate white pompadour that they should retire to a more private section of the huge mirrored room. That accomplished, Max said, "Having been with the show from the beginning I know that Tillie likes to do educational public service stories. She's treated topical subjects from gun control to teen pregnancy and has been most successful." Max paused and looked over his shoulder to make sure that no one was in hearing distance. "So I'm quite certain she'll be coming up with an AIDS story. As useful as that may be—and I know she'll treat it tastefully—I want to be sure it will not reflect on me. As you may remember a few years ago, she tackled venereal disease. At that time she wanted me, that is Dwight, to be the victim. As a pillar of society, she thought it would explore the problem with more punch. I begged her to please give the disease to another character. There's no way in the world I could face my fans—not to mention my children—with even a hint of that stigma. Many people take these stories very literally. Well, Tillie was kind enough to give the disease to someone else. Now, since you are privy to the gist of the long story in advance, I wondered if there was an AIDS story that would involve me?"

Chuck examined Max's uplifted face for a sign of understanding. "Unless your contract is up soon, I can assure you that Dwight will not be infected. Excuse me, Max. Nickie. Trudy. Where in hell is Yancey?"

"She ain't home. Just the machine," said Trudy.

"And she's not in her dressing room. The guard at the front desk hasn't seen her," Nickie added.

"One of you, go ask Clovis if he knows where she is. He was on the floor this morning but he said he was headed for Vickie's office. And let's call the next scene. We'll never get through at this rate."

Barbie Dixon, layered in approximately twenty shades of pink, looked like an inflated icecream sundae. She hovered anxiously over Clovis as he handed her the many files through which he'd riffled. She was most anxious that they were put back in the right order since Vickie Jessup was such a stickler. Handing her the last of the manila Oxford Pendaflexes, marked "Long Story–1974", he waited patiently as she carefully shoved the folder in place and readjusted its alignment. He knew she couldn't do that and talk at the same time. Finally, she gave it a last pat, closed the file drawer and turned back to Clovis.

"Barbie, you told me that you often settled bets on the show. Even between the writers. What kind of bets?"

"Oh, like whether we used a flashback in one scene or another. Sometimes it's about a character name. They start out wanting to call a character Erica and then someone will remember that she's big on ALL MY CHILDREN so they change the name so there won't be a confusion. Soap to soap. But on the earlier stories or outlines, it'll still be Erica. Often they change the name as often as three times until everyone is happy. Stuff like that," she summed up.

"You said you settled a really big disagreement between Dewey Dakin and Tillie Ryan. What was that all about?"

"That had to do with the disease," said Barbie, her round face bursting with pleasure at the depth of her knowledge.

"The disease?" asked Clovis.

"You know. Venereal. Originally they were going to give it to Dwight but Max was so worried about his image that they gave it to Dr. Milo, Lydia's son. That was to prove that even doctors got sick. We got a lot of feedback on that one."

"I'm sure you did. But what did Tillie and Dewey argue about?"

"Well," she said, revving up, "the first big story was about

murderer, Bobby Joe Meder. He was a psychotic so he only went
to the asylum, Lovely Hills, a few miles from Clearview. But the
audience loved him so much that the writers made him get well
and released him from the asylum. But Standards and Practices—
they're the Network censors—said he had to be punished more
because of his crime against society. So they gave him the disease.
And he gave it to Juanita and she gave it to Dr. Milo. Now Tillie
said that Dr. Milo cured him before he left town and became a
monk. But Dewey said he was cured *after* he left town. Of course,
she was right," Barbie said smugly.

"Barbie, I'm really impressed by your knowledge of THE KEY
TO LIFE. But why do Till and Dewey ask you rather than going
back to the scripts or tape?

"It's faster," she said simply. "There are two hundred and sixty
shows a year and the early years are in a file somewhere in New
Jersey. And we have a murder story about every three years.
Sometimes with a trial. They're great for the ratings and they take
out ads that say 'Who Killed So-and-So' and the actors get to play
really good scenes. Every now and then when there's a real murder
in the news they lift the basic story and adapt it for our characters."

"Art reflecting life," noted Clovis. And soon, he thought, we'll
have life reflecting art.

Knock and Barbie opened the door. Victoria Jessup stood there
in today's monotone. Pink. She eyed Barbie with a slight smile and
said, "We clash." Seeing Clovis, she said, "I was told to ask you if
you knew where Yancey may be. She's late and that is most
unusual."

"Damn," said Clovis, "I forgot to tell Chuck when I saw him on
the Studio floor. Yancey's going to be late today. As I understand
it, she's only in two small scenes. Yancey said she thought that the
Associate Director could stand in for her and she'll get the blocking from her when she gets here."

"I hope you haven't forgotten that we've having a story meeting in here this morning?" Vickie asked.

"No," Clovis answered, "I've been preparing for it." Vickie looked startled. "I'll go tell Chuck about Yancey. See you later."

Long Story documents on the oval table in front of them, they sat in their "assigned" seats. Dewey Dakin with his large calendars and cross-referenced script notes. Tillie beside him. Then Allie Jones, pushing her glasses and swirling her hair. Marti Livorski doodling female faces with odd hair styles. And, the new Producer, Victoria Jessup, with neatly set up legal pads and pencils and a stack of outlines. Crumbs in paper plates and empty cups testified that the amenities had been served and discussion was about to begin.

"I believe I'm pretty well caught up," Vickie began, "I've read all the new story lines. I love the one about Lydia and Dwight's long-lost brother. It's a great role but I hope we can come up with a better name for him than Oswald. It's such a wimp name."

Dewey glowered at her. "That happens to be my brother's name."

"Let's not get hung up on details," said Tillie.

The phone buzzed and Vickie picked it up. She turned to the others. "It's Clovis Kelley. He would like to join us?"

"We don't have much time," said Dewey. The others shrugged their shoulders. Allie nodded.

"Send him in," said Vickie.

Clovis opened the door and looked at all the faces turned toward him. This was not going to be easy. But then a confrontation of this sort never was. It was still, he believed, the best way to expose the murderer. Dewey's smudge brown eyes seemed opaque, Vickie lowered hers as did Marti. Tillie looked at him with interest and Allie pushed her eyeglasses once more over the bridge of her nose.

"I thank you for letting me crash your story meeting. You see, I have an interesting story line that might affect THE KEY TO LIFE. So, if you'll indulge me, I'd like to tell you the story of a murder."

"I'm fascinated," said Tillie.

"Thank you," said Clovis, leaning against the door and crossing his arms over his chest. "I think you'll all be interested in this plot. When THE KEY TO LIFE started, there was a murder story to hook and grab the audience's attention. As I see it, you set up the murders and had a killer chosen. But as you fell in love with the various characters, you kept switching the murderer. Eventually, one Bobby Joe Meder became the sacrificial victim. He was *the* murderer. A seriously disturbed man who did not even realize he had committed the crimes. Actually, the final choice of Bobby Joe was psychologically very sound." He paused. They were all now staring at him.

"Now," Clovis continued, "there are many similarites with that fictional crime and the one that took place in this Studio. The killer was a person who found it difficult to accept change of any kind. A person blinded by their own conviction that what was done *had* to be done. Therefore, there was no true guilt. Wally Krog, as you all know, was not a man who was well liked." He paused and noted Marti stopped her doodling. Allie had stopped fidgeting. "Wally had an insidious way of getting under the skin of anyone who could sense his potential evil. He would tease, torment if you will, smirking. A form of Chinese water torture. Finally, the murderer could stand it no longer and in an off moment, when Wally had given the killer the ultimate shaft, Wally got shafted."

Clovis straightened up and put his hands in his pants pockets. Five pairs of eyes stared at him. "The murderer then, when confronted by Nora the following day, gave her a karate chop that sent her to death. There were many possible people who had both the motive and the opportunity to kill Wally and I examined all of them. Each person in this room was considered. Motives ranged from blackmail by Wally to simple hatred. But there was only one person sufficiently needled to act. I followed an interesting paper trail to arrive at the person responsible for killing. I have the ultimate piece of paper right here," he said taking out the folded memo with the green doodles he had found under the sofa in the Sheraton library. "This was discarded not by Wally, as I originally thought, but by the murderer. The person to whom Wally presented this. Am I right, Mr. Dakin?"

The four women turned to stare at Dewey. A sob escaped Tillie's throat. Dewey started to shake violently. His dark eyes flashed as he said defiantly, "You can't prove a thing. You're mad!"

Tillie rose and put an arm around Dewey's trembling back. "Please go on," she said softly to Clovis.

"Let me tell you what happened. You," he addressed Dewey's lowered head, "didn't like Victoria Jessup. It had nothing to do with her work as a Producer but rather because she was a close friend of your wife's. So close that you suspected them of having a lesbian relationship." Clovis noted that Vickie blushed under her deep tan. "They had known each other from the days when DeeDee was a model and the agency for which Vickie worked handled her. As time went on, Vickie's presence made you uncomfortable and you prevailed upon Tillie to get Vickie fired." Vickie and Tillie looked at each other. No secrets here. "And at about the same time, Allie found the charming Mr. Krog who she was convinced could take Vickie's place." It was Allie's turn to blush.

"And so," Clovis continued, "Wally Krog came on the scene. But he was hardly the replacement that you had envisioned. Rude, vulgar, sarcastic, he knew how to manipulate people. That was *his* art. He got to each person in this room, with the possible exception of Vickie. Little ploys and inventions. With the ladies—yes, ladies, you cannot deny that he used flattery and sexual innuendoes to exert his power." There would be no point, Clovis knew, to be more specific. Each woman knew what Wally had done to her. Why share the pain.

"With Dewey Dakin, he used a different tack. First, he threatened his very livelihood by claiming that his wife, Betsy Simpson Krog, would make a better head writer. Obviously, anyone who knows Betsy will know that this couldn't possibly be true. But with Wally's seeming friendship with Tillie, you really started to believe that Wally could get her to remove you. The same way you had gotten Tillie to remove Vickie. And nothing that Tillie could say would change your mind." Dewey lowered his head on the table as he stopped shaking. Tillie continued to stroke his back.

"As you started to recycle a murder story line, Wally had Barbie fill him in on previous murders. He then enjoyed harping on Bobby Joe Meder and claimed that he was modelled on your family which meant that you were deranged. He would make fun of your Athletic Club affiliation, saying that real men went to the Y. None of that seemingly got to you. But it was building up and on the fatal day, he doodled on that piece of paper enclosing a 'V' and a 'D' in a heart formation. On the five minute break, when you followed him and confronted him, he allowed that he had witnessed a sex scene between your wife and Vickie."

Vickie gasped, blanching under her suntan. "That's not true. Never. Never."

"No one says that it was, Vickie," said Clovis soothingly. "But Wally was having fun testing all of Dewey's vulnerabilities. He couldn't stand Dewey's holier-than-thou attitudes and he was out to get him. He bragged about it to his then sidekick, the cameraman Frank Quinn. First Wally attacked his livelihood, then his manhood and now it was his family. And, possibly because of some deep-seated concern on Dewey's part, it was the final straw. All reason left Dewey's mind when Wally handed him the doodled paper. Dewey hid it under the sofa cusion and his hand touched the knitting needle left on the set by Maggie List. It was a lucky stroke that killed Wally but once done a great calm overcame Dewey as he convinced himself that he had done the right thing. Looking around, he realized no one had seen him. He was at peace."

"But why poor Nora?" asked Allie.

"Subconsciously, Dewey almost succeeded in erasing the deed. Much like Bobby Joe Meder. But the day of the funeral, DeeDee was working on the show and Dewey agreed to pick her up at the Studio. Ordinarily he would not have been at the Studio that day. Since DeeDee was not ready to leave, she asked him to check with the desk upstairs for her next call. He used the back staircase and ran into Nora who asked the wrong question. Possibly about Wally, maybe about DeeDee. Whatever it was, triggered his memory of what he had done. Partly from self-protection, partly from anger, he struck out at Nora. Am I right, Mr. Dakin?"

Dewey looked like all the air had been let out of him. A deflated rubber doll. He raised a tear-stained face. "She said that DeeDee was so happy Vickie was back."

"A perfectly harmless statement under any circumstance except this one. Mr. Dakin heard it as a reiteration of what Wally had said to him. He struck out," Clovis explained, "to silence her from saying anything else. To him or to anyone. It was a form of self-defense."

"What happens now?" asked Tillie.

"I've arranged to have an ambulance outside instead of a squad car. He'll be in police custody at a hospital where he can start getting the help he needs. I'm confident that the psychological ramifications will keep him out of jail."

"I'll go with him," said Tillie. "Oh, my God, someone is going to have to tell DeeDee."

"She already knows," said Clovis. "Yancey is with her."

"Pretty sure of yourself, aren't you?" said Marti as she eyed him from head to toe.

"I have to be," said Clovis.

"Thank you," fluttered Allie. "I better phone Patrick."

"Damn," said Yancey taking her make-up off in her dressing room, "there are times when the show should *not* have to go on. I feel awful. That poor man." Tears started to well in her eyes.

"How did DeeDee take it?" asked Clovis, meeting her eyes in the large make-up mirror.

"She's a trooper. And she's always known he was violently jealous of her. And unreasonably so about Vickie. It's as if he wanted to believe they had a relationship to excuse his poor performance. Turn around, I've got to get dressed and I don't trust you." Clovis turned around, a huge grin on his face. "But why did you send me to DeeDee in the first place?"

"Because I wanted to make sure you would be safe and the last place in the world Dewey would think of looking for you was his own home. I wasn't sure how he would react. And, if you'd been within striking distance here at the studio, he might have attempted to get at you. Possibly even take you hostage. You must remember that in his demented way of thinking you are an extension of me. And I am the enemy. That's why he went through all that nonsense with the telephone. Sharing your dressing room with DeeDee gave him access to the telephone book you keep here. He found the code number for your answering machine. The day you received all those hangups was Dewey wanting to try the code out. He had some addled idea that if he could get your telephone messages—especially from me —he would have an idea what I knew."

"I'm almost ready," said Yancey as she applied pale lipstick to her mouth. "But what did you mean about looking at things the wrong way."

"I kept thinking that Wally's death was directly related to his control of THE KEY TO LIFE and that 'V/D' meant venereal disease. Okay, where do you want to go?"

SHE:   What do you mean?

HE:    It's only four o'clock.

SHE:   So?

HE:    Let's go shopping.

SHE:   Where?

HE:    Your choice. Cartier or Tiffany.

SHE:   I told you what I want can't be bought there.

HE:    I thought you might change your mind.

SHE:   If it ain't broke, don't fix it.

HE:    One of these days you'll say yes.

SHE:   Maybe.

HE:    Okay. Your place or mine?

# JACQUELINE BABBIN

Jacqueline Babbin began her professional career as assistant to the noted theatrical agent Audrey Wood, who at the time represented Tennesse Williams. Babbin worked with Irene Selznick on the original Broadway production of *A Street-car Named Desire,* and then joined David Susskind as a story editor. Working on and off for Susskind over a period of fourteen years, Babbin became a full-fledged producer.

After leaving Susskind, Babbin produced for television Arthur Miller's *Memory of Two Mondays,* Lonnie Elder's *Ceremonies in Dark Old Men,* and the acclaimed series *Beacon Hill.* She then moved to Hollywood where she produced and won an Emmy for NBC's *Sybil.*

*All My Children* brought her back to Manhattan, where she was born more than a half century ago. She produced *AMC* for four and a half years before moving to Kent, Connecticut where she lives with her current breathing Ragdoll cats, Bowzer and Amos. She also lives with several hundred feline replicas: toys, paintings, statues, etc.

Jacqueline Babbin's first novel, *Bloody Special,* was recently reprinted as part of IPL's Library of Crime Classics series. She is busily at work on the third Clovis Kelley mystery.